BATMAN
MYSTERY OF THE BATWOMAN

Novelization by Louise Simonson

Based on the teleplay _Batman: Mystery of the Batwoman_
Story by Alan Burnett
Script by Michael Reaves

Batman created by Bob Kane

BANTAM BOOKS
New York • Toronto • London • Sydney • Auckland

**Visit us on the Web! www.randomhouse.com/kids
Educators and librarians, for a variety of teaching tools,
visit us at www.randomhouse.com/teachers**

Visit DC Comics at www.dckids.com

Published simultaneously in the United States and Canada

Bantam Books is an imprint of Random House Children's Books,
a division of Random House, Inc. BANTAM BOOKS and the rooster
colophon are registered trademarks of Random House, Inc.
Bantam Books, New York.

PRINTED IN THE UNITED STATES OF AMERICA

OPM 10 9 8 7 6 5 4 3 2 1

1

For the first time, she was really flying, and it felt wonderful.

She was circling one hundred and fifty feet above the freeway, crouched on her bat-shaped jet glider, balanced and in control.

Of course, she thought, anyone looking up would see her silhouette, dark against the haze-shrouded sky, bounce-lit by the lights of Gotham City.

"Let them watch, then," she muttered. "Let them learn to keep out of my way."

She spotted her target, a red Mack truck tractor hauling a car trailer stacked with tarpaulin-covered shapes—she counted seven—an everyday sight on the bustling byways of Gotham City.

The unusual element was the armed escort in the sleek black sedan following closely in the transport's wake.

She dropped through the sultry night air, skimming the river of noise and exhaust that was the Mid-Gotham Freeway, matching the sedan for course and speed.

Glancing down through the front windscreen of the sleek black vehicle, she could see two gangster types in the front

1

seat: a bald driver with chest hair sprouting like weeds from an open shirt, and a gun-toting, blond goon with short, curly hair riding shotgun. They hadn't seen her . . . yet.

Through the open window of the car, she heard the driver's muffled command: "Watch your speed, Diaz. We don't need the cops pullin' you over."

Up ahead, the truck slowed until it was moving at just below the legal speed limit.

They've got cell phones, she thought. *No surprise there.*

She dropped even lower, practically skimming the black top of the automobile. The truck driver must have asked for directions, because she heard the sedan driver answer, "You cross the bridge. Turnoff's a couple of miles beyond. Exit takes you toward the loading dock."

Ahead, she spotted the multiple-span beam bridge, just one of the many structures that crossed the Gotham River. Beyond that was a spaghetti-strand tangle of over- and underpasses.

"Right on schedule!" she said, and sped ahead, climbing to hover above the cargo carrier of the fast-moving truck.

Behind her, she heard the sedan driver's startled shout. "What's that?"

"Your worst nightmare," she snarled.

For an instant, she balanced directly above the rapidly moving trailer. Her cape cracked like a whip in the wind.

Adrenaline quickened her pulse. Blood roared in her ears. This was it. The beginning of what she had trained for, the task she had honed her mind and body to accomplish. Its outcome would mean life or death, for her and all her plans.

Her cape lifted as she leapt nimbly from her jet glider toward the middle canvas-wrapped bundle on the top rack of the car-transport frame. She spun as she landed, so that she was facing the rear of the trailer.

For a moment, she crouched there, making sure of her balance. Her bat-shaped jet glider rose into the air, where it would hover, out of harm's way, until she needed it.

Batglider's working like a dream, she thought. *Let's hope the rest of the evening goes as smoothly.*

"It's Batman!" she heard the blond goon shout. She could see the tip of his head as he leaned out the sedan's passenger window, craning his neck to get a better view.

"Close, but no cigar," she hissed.

Her crouching shape *was* dark gray, like Batman's. And she knew that the goon could see her cape, with its distinctive bat wing–like points. But he had definitely missed some important details.

Her cape was only knee length, much shorter than Batman's sweeping ankle-length cloak. And the bat-eared cowl covering her head differed from Batman's in design. While Batman's mask covered the top half of his face, a filmy covering completely obscured her entire head, except for the black-edged eyeholes.

The sedan driver spoke, sounding puzzled. "Wait, that ain't Batman!"

"Hold that thought!" she whispered. Still crouching, she pulled a triangular, knifelike object from a sheath on her belt and sliced through a cord binding the tarps.

She grabbed one side of the canvas and stood. For an instant, she was clearly silhouetted against the sky. Closer now, she heard the gangster voice shout, "Geez Louise, it *ain't* Batman! It's a Bat*woman*!"

"Bingo!" she said.

She flipped back the tarp. Beneath it, crates had been neatly stacked and strapped together to mimic the shape of a car.

Glancing down, Batwoman saw that the sedan had gained speed and pulled into the lane next to the truck. She caught a gleam of metal as the blond gangster pointed a pistol through the open window, aiming it in her direction.

She leaned forward, using her triangular blade to slash through the strap that bound the top crate shut.

"I got her in my sights," she heard the blond gunman shout. "Hold this freakin' car steady!"

2

Batwoman jerked the lid off the crate and hurled it down onto the hood of the sedan.

As the gunman opened fire, the lid ricocheted into the windshield, cracking the glass, then bounced into the road. The car swerved wildly, and the pistol blast missed Batwoman by a yard.

The crate Batwoman had opened was filled with futuristic-looking bazookas she recognized as laser blasters. She would have to destroy them, of course. But first she would deal with the muscle.

"Hold the car steady!" the fair-haired gangster snarled from the sedan window. He positioned his gun to fire again. "I almost had her!"

"Almost doesn't count," Batwoman sneered. But the sedan was running beside the hurtling truck now. Unless she acted quickly, the gunman's second shot would likely hit its mark.

Aiming carefully, Batwoman flipped the three-sided knife toward the open passenger window. The blond enforcer roared in pain and clutched his hand. The triangular blade had lodged in his wrist.

His pistol clattered harmlessly onto the freeway asphalt; then it was gone.

"What is that thing?" the bald driver shouted, glancing at his partner's bleeding wrist. "A Batarang?"

"Same principle!" Batwoman said. "But I call mine a Bat-*angle!*" In quick succession, she hurled several more toward the wheels of the car.

The Batangles struck the two right tires, which blew with loud, dramatic pops. The sedan swerved, spun wildly across several lanes, rolled upside down, and skidded sideways against the center barrier, throwing up a geyser of sparks, before sliding to a stop.

Balanced atop the transport, Batwoman half turned and glanced back toward the truck's cab. Its driver had picked up speed. He was practically flying down the freeway now.

Probably figures that the cops will be drawn to the wreck, that he's home free now, Batwoman thought. *Guess again.*

Ignoring the spectacle behind her, Batwoman lifted one of the laser blasters from its crate. Steadying it on her shoulder, she aimed it at the tarp-wrapped car shape at the rear of the trailer.

She had never fired one of these weapons, but the next step seemed obvious. She depressed the trigger.

A flash of brilliance burst from the barrel and incinerated the tarp-shrouded mound. Canvas and wood ignited.

"Sweet!" Batwoman exclaimed. Though she had thought it worth a try, she hadn't really expected the laser weapon to fire.

I can't believe those idiots are shipping these laser blasters fully armed, she thought. She had prepared a more elaborate scheme for the destruction of the weapons, but this time the bad guys had played into her hands.

"Might as well do this the easy way," she said cheerfully.

She waited an instant for the laser to recharge, then fired into a tarp-shrouded mound on the lower level of the transport.

The blast ignited that bundle—tarp, crate, weapons—as well. Through the flames, Batwoman could see that those crates had held a different sort of gun.

Batwoman felt the truck sway as the now-panicking truck driver leaned his kerchief-covered head far out the window and glanced back toward the conflagration.

He must know he's in serious trouble, Batwoman thought. *A smart dude would brake the truck and get out while he can.* Which he didn't.

That probably means the driver's more afraid of not delivering the goods than of dying in a raging inferno, she thought.

Batwoman heard the driver shout to someone in the passenger seat, "What're you sittin' there for? Get her!"

So the trucker has muscle riding with him as well, she thought. *A lot of good it's done him so far.*

Batwoman fired the blaster, igniting another bundle. She heard the passenger door creak open and a hoarse grunt as the muscle seized the grab handle outside the door. There were scuffling sounds as he inched his way over the fuel tank and hauled himself up onto the car trailer.

More than half the crates were in flames now. Batwoman didn't know whether the fire would detonate any of the weapons being hauled, and she didn't plan to stick around to find that out.

Just one more blast, Batwoman thought as she squeezed the trigger. *Then I'm out of here!*

Out the corner of her eye, she spotted movement. A dark-skinned, goatee-sporting dude, wearing a red turtleneck and beret, was balanced on the transport frame behind her, pointing a pistol.

She whipped the laser blaster around, using it like a club to knock the weapon from the gunman's hand.

Roaring angrily, the goon kicked out at her, karate-style.

Batwoman ducked to avoid the blow. Already off balance, she toppled backward, squeezing the trigger reflexively as she fell. A laser blast split the nighttime sky, disappearing quickly into the lowering smog.

She hit hard, slamming her head against the steel frame. The laser blaster flew from her nerveless hands and bounced onto the asphalt whizzing below.

That's what I get for playing nice with pond scum, Batwoman thought. *I should have offed the creep when I had the chance.*

The gunman stood over her, his red beret tilted at a jaunty angle, surrounded by the conflagration. He held a high-tech pistol at her head. "You messed with us, Bat-babe. Now you're dead!"

3

A laser blast from below flashed like lightning past the nose of the Batwing, Batman's sleek jet-driven hovercraft. For an instant, the clouds surrounding the plane were suffused with an incandescent brilliance.

So startling was the moment that Batman, who was in the forward cockpit piloting the craft, swerved reflexively, even as his brilliant mind assured him that if he could see the bolt, the danger had already passed.

Robin, Batman's teenage partner, seated in the rear navigator's seat, blinked his eyes behind his black mask, trying to clear them. The discharge had been so intense, it had even seemed to bleach the red from his costume.

He leaned forward, a shock of unruly black hair falling across his forehead as he squinted through the shrouding darkness. "Whoa, who set off the fireworks?"

"I don't know," Batman said grimly. "But I think we'd better find out."

Batman had been steering the craft by instrumentation, flying blindly through the dense, low-hanging vapor that obscured the Gotham City sky. Now, with that bright streak a ghostly afterimage on his retina, he pushed the Batwing into a dive.

The plane, with its distinctive batlike wings, emerged from the clouds above the freeway near the Gotham River. Hazy smoke veiled the scene, and Batman and Robin looked around for its source.

A mile back, an overturned sedan was in flames. Police officers, firefighters, and paramedics thronged around the vehicle. *Whatever happened there,* Batman thought, *the victims are now in good hands.*

"Smoke from that fire should have dissipated by this distance," Batman said, glancing down at his controls. "Even if the wind was blowing in this direction. Which it's not."

"Down there!" Robin said, leaning forward and almost pressing his nose against the glass. "Directly below us. A car-transport rig is also on fire."

Batman circled the Batwing so they could get a better look.

Atop a burning auto-transport trailer, half hidden by billowing smoke, a hulking figure loomed over a smaller, fallen one.

"I think the one that's down is a woman," Robin said, squinting through the haze. "Looks like she's wearing some kind of mask. The big one's a guy, and he has a gun. The woman's helpless—"

But as Robin spoke, the woman lashed out with both feet, striking the beret-wearing man squarely in the gut. He flew backward, tumbled off the truck, toppled over the bridge guardrail, and arced down, down, down until he splashed into the Gotham River.

Batman veered the Batwing toward the water, prepared to effect a rescue. But the man flailed, sputtering, to the surface. From beneath the bridge, a tugboat was chugging toward him; and as Batman and Robin watched, a sailor tossed the man a life preserver.

Batman angled the Batwing upward. Now that they knew the man was safe, they could follow the truck.

Batman saw that, while they had pursued the man, the fire had spread and now engulfed the truck's entire cargo. Through the smoke, lit by the flickering light of the flames, Batman could see the now-standing woman clearly. She wore a gray bodysuit with a red bat-shaped insignia on her chest, and her gloves were red. A mask with pointed ears covered her entire face. Her knee-length cape whipped in the wind. She was toying with the buckle of her golden hip-belt.

Robin gasped. "She's dressed like you, Batman! Cape. Hood. Similar colors."

Batman nodded grimly. "I noticed," he said.

As the Batwing glided closer, a flying jet board dropped from the clouds, accelerating smoothly until it was hovering beside the caped woman. Displaying a gymnast's grace and balance, the Batwoman leapt from the flaming cargo carrier onto the glider.

Crouching at the controls, she pulled ahead of the truck. Then she cut a hard left, turning directly in front of the truck's windshield.

Startled, the driver of the truck swerved hard and lost control of the vehicle. The cab, towing the burning trailer, crashed through the railing of the elevated freeway and soared through the air.

Batman banked the Batwing sharply. "She did that deliberately," he snarled through gritted teeth. "Set the driver up to die!"

Below the falling truck was a rutted asphalt road and a junkyard piled high with flattened metal car frames, surrounded by a chain-link fence.

Batman pressed a button, and four cable hooks shot from openings in the aircraft's undercarriage.

The hooks pierced the cab's roof and held, suspending the

cab in mid-fall. The heavier trailer, with its burning cargo, swung toward the ground. Then it ripped away and fell, smashing into the junkyard, and exploded in gouts of incandescent slag.

The cab began to swing back and forth, oscillating wildly as one of the hooks, then another, tore loose.

Looking down through the windshield of the Batwing, Robin could see the do-rag–wearing driver open his mouth in a scream of pure terror.

Acting quickly, Batman manipulated the Batwing controls, extending the remaining grapple lines, lowering the truck cab smoothly and quickly toward the rutted road beside the junkyard.

"Batman, Batwoman's back!" Robin shouted, his voice tense with excitement. "She's coming right at us!"

Batman looked up.

Batwoman hovered on her jet-driven Batglider, right in front of the Batwing. Had she wanted to, she could have reached out and touched its nose. Her mask hid the expression on her face, but her stance proclaimed both her triumph and her cool defiance. Then she rose rapidly into the clouds, leaving Batman tethered to the truck cab below.

Grim-faced, Batman watched her disappear.

Wayne Manor, a stately home belonging to billionaire playboy Bruce Wayne, nestled on a seaside estate in one of Gotham City's exclusive suburbs.

Its owner had arrived home in a state of aggravated frustration.

Now he stepped from the steamy shower into the elegant bathroom and grabbed a plush white bath sheet from the heated towel bar.

The refined voice of his butler, Alfred Pennyworth, carried

from the master bedroom beyond. "Could this woman on the glider have been an old opponent in a new disguise? Perhaps Catwoman?"

As Bruce Wayne's longtime confidant and oldest friend, Alfred was among the very few privy to his master's closely guarded secret identity.

"I don't think so!" Bruce's answer was muffled as he dried his short dark hair. "Even Selina Kyle has more regard for human life. This is someone entirely new."

Bruce emerged from the bathroom swathed in a terry cloth robe. "The last thing Gotham City needs is a vigilante running amok," he said.

Within the walk-in closet, Alfred hung an impeccably laundered blue silk shirt tailored in Hong Kong next to several others of similar hue but different fabric and designs.

"Some might say that's a bit like the kettle calling the pot black," Alfred said, a discreet smile on his face. "Anyone has the right to put on a costume. . . ."

Bruce sighed grumpily as Alfred turned to leave. "I know that, Alfred. But that Bat*woman* costume links her *to* me. What she does reflects *on* me, whether I like it or not! So who is she? What is she up to? What does she have planned? How far will she go?"

At the door to the room, Alfred turned. Light gleamed softly from his bald head as he lifted an eyebrow. "Well, do be careful, sir," he said. "Remember, there are many species in which the female is deadlier than the male."

4

Through the darkened window of his limousine, Carleton Duquesne peered with a jaundiced eye at Beak's Bric-A-Bracs factory. It was a vaulting building, with three rows of windows, built of cinderblocks and looking, from the outside, as if it were three stories tall. Its logo, the abstract head of a bird with an open beak, reminded Duquesne of the factory's notorious owner, known to everyone as the Penguin.

Recently, Carleton Duquesne had tied his hopes to that flightless bird's tail. He just hoped he wouldn't wind up buried in Penguin poop.

The limousine pulled through the gate of a chain-link fence topped with barbed wire, into the factory loading area in the back of the building.

Duquesne saw that his other partner, Rupert Thorne, was waiting beside the loading platform. Thorne was nothing special. Just your average, middle-aged, slightly overweight tough-guy criminal kingpin.

A lot like me, Duquesne thought. *Except Thorne still has a healthy mane of thick white hair.* Duquesne ran his hand over his own smooth bald head. His only hair was on his face—a black mustache and Vandyke beard.

"And Thorne still loves what we do," Duquesne muttered. Unlike him, Thorne was still at the top of his game.

Through hard, beady eyes, Thorne watched as Duquesne's limo pulled to a stop. Thorne's fleshy face, with its bent nose that looked like it had been rearranged by the blunt end of a shovel, was expressionless. Only his fingers flashed nervously as he shuffled a deck of cards with one hand.

Lord, I'm tired of all this garbage, Duquesne thought. *Why can't things ever just go as planned?*

Duquesne's stomach was hurting again. Shielded by the dark window, he popped a couple more antacids, then washed them down with a swig of bottled water.

Duquesne's driver opened the rear passenger door. As Duquesne climbed out, he schooled his face into a tough, impassive mask, mirroring Thorne's.

Like a sleight-of-hand artist, Thorne caused the king of clubs to rise to the top of the deck. Then he reshuffled, thumbing the cards with a loud *zip* before pocketing them.

"The Penguin's been waiting," Thorne said.

He led the dark-skinned Duquesne up the loading dock steps, past workers piling crates onto a truck, and into the Bric-A-Bracs factory.

As its name implied, Beak's Bric-A-Bracs produced bird-related kitsch—everything from lawn flamingos to plastic parrot key chains.

Thorne and Duquesne walked silently through several assembly lines with moving conveyor belts and pounding machinery, then past a long table where white-haired ladies sat painting details onto bird-shaped piggy banks.

As the gangsters approached an inset door without handles, Thorne produced a key card. He slipped it into a slot beside the entrance, and the door slid open.

Thorne and Duquesne stepped through the aperture into an elevator.

The doors slid shut, and the elevator began to sink. As it slid smoothly beneath the upper floor, the passengers became aware that the elevator walls were transparent.

Even knowing what was coming, every time he saw the place, Duquesne was impressed anew with the Penguin's audacity. The supposedly retired and reformed criminal mastermind had constructed another factory—a munitions plant—in the sub-subbasement below Bric-A-Bracs.

While sweet little ladies painted smiles above, below hardnosed thugs were clamping, screwing, and sealing parts into the bazooka-like laser blasters and other weapons that, Duquesne hoped, would provide for his own retirement and, when the time came, create a legacy he could leave his only daughter.

From their platform vantage point, Thorne and Duquesne spotted the author of this operation—the short, unimposing, rotund, pointy-nosed Oswald Chesterfield Cobblepot, who called himself the Penguin.

The Penguin was dressed impeccably in a black tuxedo coat, a bow tie, a top hat, white gloves, and old-fashioned spats. In his right eye socket, he wore a monocle.

On anyone else, the getup would have looked over-the-top, even clownlike, Duquesne thought. *But the Penguin pulled it off.*

And there was nothing comical about his credentials, or his agenda. The Penguin was one of Gotham City's most infamous criminal geniuses—highly energetic, inventive, ever on the prowl for new ways to subvert the system and get even richer than he already was.

Most of the time he let others do his dirty work for him. He himself was seldom apprehended.

The Penguin, temporarily ignoring the approach of his partners, stood beside a firing range, aiming one of his trademark deadly umbrellas at a cardboard silhouette of Batman. His white-gloved finger depressed a button on the umbrella handle, and its pointed tip launched like a missile. It struck the cardboard, blowing off the right half of the cutout's head.

The Penguin turned to the lab-coated technician accompanying him.

"You see," he complained, handing the tech the umbrella. "It still lists to the right. See what you can do."

As the technician nodded and backed away, Duquesne called out, "Penguin!"

The Penguin turned to face his partners. His expression was cold, his voice tight and unfriendly. "Mr. Duquesne. I hear we had an unpropitious setback."

Duquesne cleared his throat. "If you mean we got hit, yeah, you could say that."

"And how exactly could that have happened?" the Penguin asked, his voice silky.

Duquesne shrugged uncomfortably. "I dunno yet," he said. "No one but us even knew the shipment was goin' out last night."

The Penguin raised an eyebrow above his monocle. "Well, obviously *someone* knew."

Thorne fanned out his cards, chuckling derisively. "Yeah," he said. "But a bat *woman*?"

Duquesne scowled. "That's what my man said, Thorne."

*   *   *

"Bat man, Bat girl, Bat woman . . . ," the Penguin grumbled. "What *is* it about this city? The *water*?"

He picked up a new umbrella from a display case and began to saunter toward his downstairs office. Thorne and Duquesne followed.

"Fortunately, we only lost one truckload," Duquesne said. "I've doubled the manpower at our warehouse sites. No way she can get to the rest."

"Forgive me if I'm not so sanguine," the Penguin said, gesturing with his umbrella for emphasis. "Our overseas consortium has already paid us half up front—a half *billion* dollars for these arms. If we don't deliver, they'll want their money back. And since we used most of it to capitalize the arms plant, that would present a problem, wouldn't it, gentlemen?"

The Penguin stopped and turned, squinting up into Duquesne's face. "I want the rest of the delivery to be out of Gotham within the week, which means you'd better take care of this bat clone now."

Pointing his umbrella at Duquesne's chest, he continued, "You're supposed to be our muscle, Mr. Duquesne. Start flexing!"

The Penguin turned on his heels and stalked off. Duquesne stared after him and frowned. No one wanted this venture to succeed more than he did. He would just have to make sure nothing else went wrong.

5

Between the destruction of the arms shipment, his meeting with the Penguin, and more bad news concerning his other capital ventures, Duquesne was not having a good day.

He sat at the desk in his penthouse home office, phone to his ear, listening to yet another denial of responsibility. As his guts clenched spasmodically, he reached for an antacid bottle and shook several pills into his hand.

Duquesne owned real estate, of course, including the towering building in which he lived. His penthouse office, with its Dark Deco–designed French doors, overlooked a patio and pool. Beyond them spread downtown Gotham City. Here, at least, he was king.

But his investments—particularly his heavy holdings in tech stocks—had evaporated, and several of his real estate ventures were in trouble.

If the weapons deal didn't pay off big, he could lose everything.

"Well, someone talked," Duquesne snarled into the telephone. "Somebody dropped a dime! We find out who, we'll find *her*—

"Hold on a minute," he ordered as he heard the penthouse elevator slide open.

Through the French doors that led to his office, Duquesne watched as his daughter, Kathy, strode into the foyer. She was in her early twenties, with spiky black hair and skin the color of brown sugar. She reminded him so much of her mother at that age. Her beautiful mother, who had been killed. Because of him. From that point, his life had taken a downhill slide.

He popped the antacids into his mouth and washed them down with a swig from his water bottle.

Two gangster types—blond, hulking Wilbur and slick, dark-skinned Chic—trailed after his daughter, their arms piled high with packages and hatboxes. Both men had more muscle than brains, but they made impressive-looking bodyguards. And, even though Kathy resented their constant presence, so far they'd kept his headstrong baby girl safe.

Kathy opened the French doors and sauntered into his office. Wilbur and Chic trudged behind her, laden like bearers on a safari.

Kathy was wearing a designer outfit made by some Italian guy Duquesne couldn't remember the name of—a gold silk dress and fitted jacket, with matching shoes and purse. She looked like a million bucks . . . approximately what the outfit had cost him. Duquesne sighed.

My daughter has good taste, he thought proudly. *Expensive taste.* Yet another reason this latest venture had to succeed.

"Where you been?" Duquesne asked, leaning back in his chair and scowling up at his elegant, long-limbed daughter.

Kathy shrugged a shoulder. "Shopping, of course. Don't worry, Daddy. I took your lapdogs with me when I went out. For once, they came in handy."

She faced the two tough guys. "Give Donna my packages. She'll know what to do with them."

As they turned to go, a hatbox nearly toppled to the floor. Kathy caught it and put it back atop Wilbur's pile.

"Shoo!" Kathy dismissed them with a wave of her hand.

She sashayed toward her father. "So. Raoul, my favorite hairdresser, had a spiritual rebirth and left for an ashram in Bukittinggi. I'm distraught. How was your day?"

Duquesne ignored the question. "You should tell me when you go out."

"Uh-huh!" As Kathy leaned down to give his clean-shaven head a daughterly peck, she noticed the lit call line. "Looks like I interrupted a conversation. Sorry. Who's on the phone?" she asked.

"Business," Duquesne said brusquely. "Nothing for you to worry about."

Kathy stepped back. "Well, then. I guess I should be going," she huffed, and stalked away.

At the office door, she turned and glanced back. "If I hung around, we might be forced to have an actual conversation."

She fluttered her fingers and uttered her trademark exit line: "Ta-ta!"

Then she was gone.

Duquesne sighed. *What's wrong with the girl?* he asked himself. Why did she always seem so angry? So . . . rebellious. He gave her everything she wanted. Why couldn't she just be happy?

I don't understand her, he thought sadly.

Duquesne picked up the phone, and his expression hardened. "Do whatever it takes. I want you to find that Batwoman," he said. "Find her and *finish* her!"

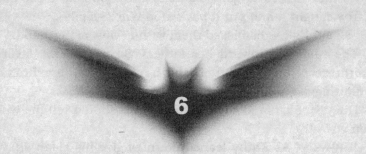

6

Bruce Wayne leaned back against the plush leather seat of the limousine and clicked the TV remote.

"Give it up, Bruce. It won't do you any good to keep switching channels," Tim Drake, Bruce Wayne's teenage ward, said from the seat beside him. "The news on every local station is more or less the same."

Not bothering to look up from the comic book he was reading, Tim mimicked a particularly annoying female reporter's breathy voice. "All of Gotham is wondering who the mysterious Batwoman is. . . . Is she Batman's new partner? Batgirl, grown up? Blah, blah, blah."

Ignoring Tim, Bruce clicked the TV remote once again.

This channel showed an irritable-looking Police Commissioner James Gordon, surrounded by shoving, shouting reporters.

"All I can tell you is that this so-called Batwoman is not affiliated with Batman. Otherwise I have no comment," Gordon snapped.

"See," Tim said. "*He* knows nothing. *Nobody* knows anything. Including *us!*"

Bruce clicked again moodily.

A black-haired man with a face like a mashed potato appeared on the TV screen. Beneath the image, an identifying line across the bottom of the screen read, *Sgt. Harvey Bullock, G.P.D.*

Bullock—tall, broad, built like a sumo wrestler, and never the picture of sartorial elegance—looked even grumpier and more rumpled than usual.

"I think we got more than enough bat-freaks in Gotham already," he said. "I mean, sheesh, what's next—*Bathound*?"

"Funny he should mention that." Tim looked up from his comic, eyes twinkling. "I've been *thinking* about getting a dog. He could help us sniff out clues!"

Bruce gave him a withering look. Then, when his cell phone rang, Bruce sighed, switched off the TV, and answered, "Bruce Wayne here."

"Bruce, it's Barbara," said a chipper female voice.

Barbara. Commissioner Gordon's teenage daughter. Bruce closed his eyes. He could feel a headache coming on.

"Hey, Barb," he said.

Tim batted his eyelashes at Bruce. "She misses you," he sang in a lilting voice.

Bruce ignored him. "How's college?" he asked.

"Not bad," Barbara said. "But the nightlife here can't compare with kicking butt as Batgirl."

Then her voice turned seductive. "But spring break will be coming up soon and I'll be back in Gotham for two whole weeks. Won't that be nice?"

Bruce shifted uncomfortably. "Yes, we'll *all* be happy to see you," he said.

Tim buried his nose in his comic. "Hey, don't drag *me* into this," he said.

"Anyway, that's not the reason I called," Barbara continued.

"I just saw the news, and I was wondering if you'd gotten a new partner. Someone a little . . . older?"

Bruce jumped in. "I have no idea who this woman is. Really, Barb."

Barbara talked over his denial. " 'Cause if you had, I'd be really upset. I thought you and I were, you know—"

Desperate to end this conversation, Bruce grabbed a piece of paper from his open briefcase and crumpled it beside the phone, simulating static.

"Uh, Barb, we're going through the East . . . Tunnel now . . . ," he said, pretending the signal was breaking up. "Talk . . . later . . ."

Quickly, Bruce pressed the button that ended the call. He sat back, feeling relieved.

"Squeaked through again, didn't ya?" Tim teased him.

Alfred, who was acting as chauffeur that morning, glanced at Bruce in the rearview mirror.

"I never fail to marvel at your narrow escapes, sir," he said with feigned admiration.

As the limousine eased to a stop in front of the Wayne Enterprises building, Bruce put away his cell phone and snapped his briefcase shut.

"It's not like I ever lead her on." He looked out the window moodily. "And right now, I have enough female bat problems as it is."

"You sure I can't cut school?" Tim said as Bruce climbed from the car. "I'd really like to see Dr. Ballentine's presentation. She's awesome."

"She is," Bruce agreed. "That's why Wayne Industries has employed her. Her work in metallurgy is spectacular. I didn't realize you were interested—"

"I'm not . . . exactly," Tim admitted with a shrug. "She also holds the national championship for number of points

24

accrued in the Space Freaks video game! Among gamers, Rocky Ballentine is a legend."

"You had me worried there for a minute," Bruce said. "You're not missing much this morning. The meeting will be a boring technical presentation attended by a bunch of suits."

Tim grinned. "Here's a flash, Bruce! Here and now, *you're* the biggest suit of all!"

Bruce laughed. "No need to get insulting! Drop by after school and I'll introduce you to Dr. Ballentine!"

7

She doesn't look like a legend, Bruce thought as he stared at the freckle-faced young woman with flyaway blond hair. *Or a metallurgical genius either.* She looked, in fact, like an overgrown pixie.

Roxanne "Rocky" Ballentine wasn't yet twenty-five years old. She stood in the boardroom of Wayne Enterprises, before a series of easels, with large presentation cards displaying esoteric data in graph format, and her inexperience in speaking to nonscientist "suits" was obvious.

"So as you can see," Rocky said, tapping a card with the pointer she held in her hand, "the alloy's tensile malleability is remarkably high, given its density and homeotropic structure—"

The easel Rocky touched wobbled dramatically, and she made a frantic grab, snagging it before it fell, but knocking into another.

From the glazed looks in the eyes of the Wayne Enterprises businesspeople, they found her explanations near-incomprehensible. Rocky obviously realized that she had lost her audience but had no idea how to regain their attention.

Grimly, she shoved the display card beneath her arm, where she had amassed a slippery collection of already-used charts. The diagrams slid dangerously, and she struggled to shift them back into order, even as she tried to keep the presentation on target.

"Meaning that...uh...the flexible molecular stacking will..."

Rocky glanced back nervously as the chart on the easel behind her began to careen toward the floor.

"Uh...provide considerable morphological adaptability..."

There was a *Whap!* as the chart hit the ground and toppled into the easel beside it.

"Um...through the electromagnetic..."

Bruce could tell the exact moment when Rocky realized that all the easels were going to go down like a house of cards. She started speaking more rapidly, trying to get the words out before her entire presentation literally fell apart.

". . . manipulationofthequantumstates!" She ran the words together frantically as cards and easels clattered to the floor in a dramatic finale.

For a moment, Rocky stood before the "suits" looking like she wanted to crawl under the plush boardroom carpet.

Then she stuck out her chin. With sudden decisiveness, she dropped the pointer and the charts and walked over to a nearby table. On it rested a softball-sized sphere of silver metal.

She held the metal out toward her audience.

"See this chunk of metal?" she asked. "I've programmed it to change shape. Watch!"

She snatched a pencil from the boardroom table and tapped the top of the metal.

Instantly, the alloy morphed, splitting into petals until it formed a flowerlike shape.

Electric excitement galvanized the executives. They sat mesmerized as she tapped another point, and the petals closed, forming a perfect pyramid.

She tapped a third point, and the sides flared up, creating an abstract butterfly.

Another tap, and it became a small replica of the Statue of Liberty.

The awestruck executives, unable to contain their excitement, broke into tumultuous applause.

Rocky beamed, with pleasure and—Bruce thought, amused—with relief that the presentation was now over.

Her smile was nearly irresistible. Bruce couldn't help grinning back.

Bruce was pleased when the young scientist agreed to have dinner with him that evening.

They were eating at Swank's, a retro, 1960s-style restaurant. Seated at a window table lit softly by neon light, they speared cubes of delicious French bread with long forks, then dipped them into a small pot of richly spiced melted cheese, kept hot over a tiny burner.

It was a business dinner filled mainly with shop talk, but Bruce found that he very much enjoyed her quirky intelligence and her slightly off-kilter personality.

"Actually the technology's pretty simple. It's just a matter of imprinting morph lines with a pressure point," Rocky explained. "I'm not even sure what it's good for."

Bruce smiled. "I happen to have a, uh, 'silent partner' who I'm sure will find some use for it."

Rocky sighed. "That's great." She speared a cube of bread with her fork. "I can't tell you how cool it is to be in an R and D company that takes young women seriously." She dipped the bread cube into the fondue mixture. "Especially blondes."

Bruce raised his eyebrows. "At WayneTech, it's what's under the hair that counts, Dr. Ballentine."

"It's Rocky," she said, waving the cheese-covered bread expressively. "Actually Roxanne, but people have always called me Rocky for some reason—"

She broke off as the bread cube flew off her waving fork and smacked into the window. "Oh, no!"

She shut her eyes, as if not wanting to see the smear the cheese left on the window.

"Look! Up in the sky! It's the Bat-Signal!" a voice from the table behind them called out.

Rocky and Bruce stared up through the fondue-smudged window. The Bat-Signal was, indeed, projected against the evening clouds.

Rocky's eyes widened in amazement. "Wow! I've never seen it before! Isn't it exciting?"

Bruce gave her a wan smile. "Every time!" he said.

With a sigh of regret for the end of an enjoyable evening, he signaled the waiter to bring their check.

8

Atop the roof of the Gotham City Police Headquarters, Commissioner James Gordon was waiting next to the spotlight that was projecting the Bat-Signal onto the evening clouds. Standing a bit behind him were the ever-rumpled Sergeant Harvey Bullock and Detective Sonia Alcana.

As he waited for Batman to arrive, Bullock nonchalantly twirled a key chain back and forth on his finger. Bullock was an old hand at waiting for Batman.

By contrast, Sonia Alcana was anything but nonchalant. She shifted on her feet, impatiently checked her watch, then gazed into the sky expectantly.

"He'll get here," Bullock told Alcana in a bored voice. "And remember, when he does, *I'll* do the talkin'."

Sonia's amber eyes flashed as she glanced at Bullock and tossed back her shoulder-length auburn hair. She knew his type, faced them every day on the job. They came with the territory when you were a woman cop.

Idly, she glanced behind them, and her eyes widened. Behind Bullock, Batman swung in on a bat-line, emerging from the night like a living shadow. His billowing cape added to his ghostly quality and to the unquestionable drama of his entrance.

Batman landed and approached Commissioner Gordon.

"What is it, Commissioner?" he asked.

"I had Bullock collect the remains of the contraband Batwoman destroyed two nights ago," Gordon said, gesturing to a lab table on wheels, which held the charred remains of different types of incinerated firearms. "I thought you might like to take a look."

Batman gazed down at the weaponry. Even burned and slagged, the shapes of many of the weapons were bizarre and futuristic-looking. Batman lifted one of the larger firearms and studied it carefully.

Bullock stepped forward, still twirling the key chain.

"Stuff's outta *Star Trek*," he said. "Looks to me like someone broke into a toy store. . . ."

Batman frowned. "These aren't toys, Bullock. This is a plasma rifle. It can take out a tank at two hundred yards."

"More like five hundred," Sonia Alcana interjected.

Batman raised a questioning eyebrow.

Sonia shrugged. "I measured the clip size."

Commissioner Gordon nodded toward her. "Sonia Alcana. Bullock's new partner," he said.

Ignoring Bullock's scowl as she took center stage, Sonia pointed out other weapons. "There's also a couple of E-K-4 lasers, an infra-beam bazooka, and what looks like the barrel from a surface-to-air missile launcher."

Batman glanced over the weapons and nodded approval. "Any idea who's behind this?"

Bullock twirled the key chain. "The truck driver ain't talking, but I got some leads. Can't say anything definite right now. . . ."

Sonia glanced at Bullock disparagingly. "In other words, we have nothing," she said.

Suddenly, Batman's hand shot out and snatched the twirling keys from Sergeant Bullock's finger.

"Hey!" Bullock shouted, then fell silent as Batman studied the key chain.

Batman gave Bullock a hard glance. "Where did you get this?" he asked sternly.

Bullock scowled, on the defensive. "From the guy's truck, when I had it impounded. What about it?"

Batman looked at the rumpled policeman as if he were the sorriest excuse for a cop on the planet. Then he tossed the keys back to Bullock.

Batman turned to Commissioner Gordon. "I'll get back to you!" he said.

He fired off a grappling hook toward a nearby building. Holding on to the line, he leapt from the roof, disappearing into the shadows like the creature of the night that he was.

As Bullock glared after the exiting Batman, Sonia reached over and lifted the keys from his palm.

Dangling from the keys was a circular piece of plastic with an abstract drawing of a bird's head with its beak opened wide.

Several hours later, the sleekly curved Batmobile pulled quietly into an alley adjacent to Beak's Bric-A-Bracs factory.

The building windows were dark. The loading dock was empty. The factory was silent as a grave.

"Looks like Bric-A-Bracs is closed for the night," Robin said, studying the building through the Batmobile's windshield. "The Penguin owns this place?"

"Along with Duquesne and Thorne," Batman answered.

Batman and Robin climbed from the car. Batman pulled binoculars from his Utility Belt.

"Nice triumvirate of crooks," Robin said. He studied the factory with its bird logo curiously. "What do they make here?"

"Trinkets, figurines," Batman answered. "And weapons of mass destruction."

Batman focused the binoculars beyond the barbed-wire-topped fence that surrounded the loading yard, and he studied the factory building carefully.

The exterior cinderblock walls featured three rows of windows, positioned to make use of available natural light, and the roof held a row of skylights.

"I don't see any of the Penguin's goons around," Robin said, scanning the parking lot and loading docks beyond.

Then the *pop-pop-pop* of gunfire made him jump. "It's coming from inside the building," Robin whispered.

But Batman had already leapt atop the Batmobile and was firing a grapnel-tipped line over the fence, up toward Bric-A-Brac's high roof. It caught on a gutter, and Batman flew up into the air.

Robin followed close behind.

9

"There she is," shouted one of the thugs who were chasing her.

Looking back, Batwoman could barely make out the shape of a gun-toting goon silhouetted against a window.

"I see her," another voice called from the left. "I think I winged her."

In your dreams, Batwoman thought. *Still, I can't let this go on too long. I've got to get out of here.*

She picked up the pace as she ran through aisles of oddly shaped silhouettes, all she could see of the factory machinery. The vague brightness coming through the rows of factory windows and the skylights did little to illuminate the plant's interior.

Batwoman ducked and rolled beneath a table. She came to a stop, crouching behind a tall stack of crates, listening for approaching footsteps.

The thugs came pelting up, then stopped, turning in circles, eyes no doubt straining to spot her in the dark.

"You see her?" one of them asked, sounding confused.

You'd think they'd have enough sense to switch on the lights,

Batwoman thought. *Guess I'm lucky they have more brawn than brains.*

Or maybe they have orders not to do anything that will draw attention to this place. Batwoman grinned. *Good luck with that one after tonight.*

She stood suddenly and shoved the crates with all her might. The heavy boxes toppled toward the goons. She heard a startled shout, a burst of gunfire. Then a loud clatter as the crates crashed on top of the gangsters.

The gunman shouted, "I dropped my blasted pistol!"

That evens the odds a bit, Batwoman thought, and looked around for the exit.

"There she is!" a voice to her left shouted. She glanced left. More goons were clambering over a conveyor belt to get at her. Only the lead goon in that crew had a gun.

Batwoman lunged for a control panel and hit a button, and the assembly line activated. The belt began to advance, throwing the gunman and his cohorts off balance. They toppled onto the moving belt. Nearby a nozzle swiveled, spraying them with thick enamel paint.

Batwoman was dashing for the exit when the three goons who had been felled by the crates stepped in front of her, blocking her path. One thug held a chain; she could see its dark, unmistakable shape. Another held a section of pipe.

She turned to race the other way. The paint-covered creeps from the conveyor belt blocked her path. Several held cudgels. The lead goon had a gun pointed right at her heart.

Suddenly, a Batarang struck the gunman's hand. He dropped his weapon, howling angrily.

Batman and Robin swung down from the skylight above and landed next to Batwoman.

"Why don't we even the sides a bit?" Robin said.

"Get 'em!" the leader shouted, and the thugs, quickly getting over their shock, rushed at the heroes.

"Welcome to super-hero team-up!" Robin quipped.

Batman and Batwoman fought side by side as if they had been partners for years. Robin, his back to the others, held his own.

"Not that I'm not grateful," Batwoman said, "but you shouldn't be here!"

Batwoman ducked a swinging chain and kicked out at a goon, sending him crashing back into the paint-spraying machine.

Batman dodged a cudgel and punched his assailant in the gut. "Look who's talking," he grunted.

"No. I mean, I've set a charge," Batwoman said urgently.

Batman ducked a swinging pipe, then side-kicked his attacker. "Where?" he asked.

A final goon came at Batwoman. She flipped him over her shoulder. "Below us," she said. "There's a munitions room. The bomb isn't big, but it will be very effective."

"When will it—" Batman began. His question was interrupted by a *hisss*...then a *whumph!* that shook the building. All around the combatants, sections of the floor shot skyward on geysers of flame.

The windows and skylights blew outward in shards of glass.

"Duck!" Batwoman shouted. Batman and Robin obeyed her, diving aside as the door of the metal elevator that had led to the subbasement hurtled over their heads and slammed into the assembly machinery.

Black smoke was seeping up everywhere. The factory was now in flames.

One of the goons scrambled to his feet, shouting, "Let's get outta here!"

The other goons stumbled upright and, half carrying their semiconscious partner, lumbered toward the door.

Batman and Robin looked around. Batwoman had dis-appeared.

"Where'd she go?" Robin asked, exasperated.

Batman glanced up toward the blown-out skylight. "Check the door," he said. "I'll see if she fled onto the roof."

Robin dashed for the door as Batman fired his grappling hook, then rose toward the ceiling.

10

Batman grabbed the edge of the skylight, grateful to be wearing gloves to protect his hands from shards of glass, and lifted himself onto the roof. Smoke was billowing up from the basement level, escaping through windows and skylights. Soon, Batman knew, the upper factory would be engulfed in flames. Then the whole structure would collapse.

He looked around. Where was Batwoman?

Her voice sounded from behind him. "They were manufacturing arms for Kaznia, something I'm sure the State Department would frown upon."

Not to mention NATO and the United Nations, Batman thought. The last thing that war-torn nation steeped in years of ethnic strife needed was an infusion of arms...especially arms as lethal as those that had been manufactured in the factory below.

Batwoman turned to face Batman as she continued. "This was their weapons plant."

"I figured that out," Batman said. "But it will be a little hard to prove now."

He nodded toward the smoke and said, "By the time the fire is out, everything here will be slag and twisted metal."

Batwoman shrugged. "Doesn't matter. *They're* finished here." There was the hint of a victorious smile behind her gauzy face mask. "But *I've* just begun."

She turned to leave, but Batman grabbed her arm, stopping her.

"Who are you?" he growled. "Why are you doing this?"

Behind the mask, her smile changed to a sneer. "You're the great detective, Batman. You figure it out!" she said.

She jerked sideways, and expertly using Batman's own momentum against him, she flipped him over her shoulder.

Batman landed on his feet and sprang toward her.

"Deft," she said. "You're no slouch!"

Batwoman sent a series of jabs toward Batman's midsection. He blocked them, then aimed a spinning kick at her head. It was her turn to duck backward.

"Guess this is what you'd call a standoff," she said. She touched her belt control as she took a step backward.

"Hate to fight and run, but—" With a perfectly coordinated back flip, Batwoman leapt off the roof and disappeared.

Batman made it to the edge in time to see Batwoman's glider zoom beneath her. With the precision of an Olympic gymnast, she landed crouching on the board.

The jet glider moved off into the night.

"Not so fast," Batman said sharply. He had a few more questions for this self-styled Batwoman.

He whipped out his grappler and fired it upward.

The clamp at the end sunk its metal teeth into the glider. Batman jerked with all his strength . . . and was lifted high into the air.

* * *

Standing in the parking lot beyond the burning factory building, Robin glanced around, noting that the Penguin's enforcers had all disappeared. They probably knew some way out of the fenced parking area that he did not.

Catching a flash of movement overhead, Robin looked up. Batman was swinging on a cable attached to Batwoman's jet glider as she rose high over Gotham City.

Robin fired his own cable-attached grapnel hook at the building across the alley where the Batmobile was parked. Hitting the retractor button, he was pulled up over the chain-link fence.

Robin swung over the alley, landed, feet braced, against the brick wall, then dropped beside the Batmobile. He leapt inside and gunned the motor, and the Batmobile roared dramatically to life.

I'll try to follow, try to keep them in sight, Robin thought as he thundered from the alley and turned onto the cross street. But already he could see it was hopeless. Batman and Batwoman were darker specks, now, against the midnight sky.

Then, when the Batmobile screeched around a corner, a tall building came between Robin and his quarry. He had lost them.

11

Batman was being hauled through the air, a thousand feet over Gotham, hanging by the thinnest of cables from a flying board.

It's thin, but it's strong, he thought. His equipment had withstood the test of time. That wouldn't be a problem.

Batman pressed the rewind button on the grapnel and the line retracted, hauling him up toward the woman balanced gracefully on her glider.

She has to know I'm down here, Batman thought. *The question is, what is she going to do about it?*

Batwoman rose on her Batglider, until she was flying level with the roofs of Gotham's highest skyscrapers.

Of course, she had noted the drag on her jet board, Batman realized. Now she would feel the faint vibration as the retractable line hauled Batman up toward her.

As Batman was pulled closer to the glider, he saw Batwoman's head turn as she looked down at him. He didn't need to see her face to tell what she was feeling. Her whole body radiated irritation.

"Naughty, naughty," she said softly. "When a lady says no, she means *no!*"

Batman had nearly reached the jet board when she pulled a Batangle from her belt pouch and hurled it at the grapnel line. The spinning triangular blade sliced through the tough cable as if it were silken thread.

Suddenly, Batman found himself falling. But because he was so far up in the air, he had time to act. Whipping a cable-connected Batarang from his belt pouch, he scanned the buildings below, searching for a likely target.

There! He spotted a flagpole held in the hands of a grinning gargoyle.

He threw the Batarang. It spun several times around the gleaming metal shaft. Batman swung down holding the cord. As his weight pulled the cable taut, the knot caught. And held.

Batman swung in a long arc across the Dark Deco cityscape and landed on the roof of a nearby skyscraper.

Standing atop one of the city's taller buildings, he had an uninterrupted view of much of downtown Gotham.

He whipped his binoculars from his belt pouch and looked around for Batwoman. He scanned the sky at increasingly greater magnification, but she had apparently disappeared.

Grimly, he switched his scan to heat-sensing infrared.

There! he thought. *An orange moving dot that big, that warm, that high. It has to be Batwoman!*

He zoomed in on the dot, tracking it with his greatest possible magnification. *Yes,* he thought. *Definitely human shaped.*

It seemed to disappear behind the top of a skyscraper.

That's Duquesne's building. He lives in the penthouse with his daughter, Batman thought. *So what is Batwoman up to now?*

* * *

Moments later, Batman had almost reached Duquesne's towering, ultramodern-looking building.

At the end of a cable line, he arced into the air, fired another grapnel toward the ledge of Duquesne's penthouse terrace, and pushed the retract button.

Batman was pulled upward toward the lush and elaborate terrace garden.

He climbed over the parapet and landed in a clump of concealing shrubbery.

From the open window of Duquesne's office came a gruff exclamation. "Who? The Batwoman?"

Batman edged toward the penthouse. Standing in its shadow, beside the open window, he peered inside.

Duquesne was sitting at his desk, facing the French doors that led to the foyer. His back was toward Batman.

"What do ya mean it's gone?" Duquesne snarled into the receiver. "The whole building?"

Behind Batman, there was a faint crunch of gravel, the barest whisper of clothing brushing against shrubbery.

From the corner of his eye, Batman saw a large, blond, muscle-bound thug take a cautious step toward him, cudgel upraised.

Without bothering to turn, Batman, reaching back and upward, grabbed the goon's upraised wrist—hard.

The goon let out a yelp of pain.

Batman stood, turned, and hit the thug with a karate chop to the side of his neck.

The thug crumpled into the shrubbery.

Drawn by the outcry, three more goons raced toward Batman.

"Watch it, Chic," a bodyguard snarled toward a dapper black man. "He flattened Wilbur like a bug!"

Ignoring the advice, Chic leapt at Batman.

Batman crouched, eyes narrowed. *Come and get it, then,* he thought. After his frustrating pursuit of Batwoman, he realized, he was relishing the opportunity for a fight.

Duquesne looked up, phone in hand, as Chic crashed through the double doors that led to the terrace and skidded, face first, across the floor.

"I'll call you back!" Duquesne snarled into the phone.

He shoved back his chair, stalked around his desk, stepped over Chic, crunched through broken glass, and threw his shattered terrace doors open.

Batman stood on his terrace. Four of Duquesne's men were on the ground around him, in various states of consciousness.

"You got a lot of nerve, freak!" Duquesne growled. "Haven't you and your woman caused me enough grief tonight?"

Beneath Duquesne's rant, Batman heard another, softer sound. He glanced up quickly. A woman was watching from the residential section above, standing a bit back from an open window. He could see her vague outline, the glitter of her eyes, but little else.

"This is my home," Duquesne roared. "You're bothering my family! Get out!"

Batman glanced at Duquesne, assessing. Then, for the briefest instant, his gaze held that of the woman in the window.

Then he turned and vaulted over the edge of the terrace, firing his grappler as he leapt.

12

It was one of those rare summer mornings in Gotham City when the sky was near-cloudless and the sun warmed the terrace outside Duquesne's penthouse office.

The wreckage from the confrontation of the night before had been cleared away, and the terrace doors had already been replaced.

Duquesne was sitting outside his office at a glass-topped table covered with a snowy-white tablecloth. His breakfast plate was piled high with eggs, waffles, ham, sausage, bacon, and hash browns.

Daddy doesn't look like he's enjoying either the weather or that mound of food, Kathy Duquesne thought as she sauntered onto the terrace.

"Having your usual continental breakfast, Daddy?" she asked from right behind him.

Since Kathy was little that had been one of their private jokes . . . that his breakfasts were as big as continents, therefore they were continental breakfasts. But then, when she was small, they both would laugh at the silly, oft-repeated banter.

Carleton Duquesne wasn't laughing now. He grunted grumpily and shoved another bite of ham into his mouth.

Kathy sat opposite him in the sunshine and daintily picked up a raspberry croissant. She looked at her father curiously.

"I heard a commotion last night," she said. "Who was here?"

"Nobody." Duquesne finished chewing, then washed the bite down with a gulp of coffee.

Kathy glanced toward Wilbur and Chic, who were standing guard at the terrace doors.

"Wilbur," she said in mock shock. "You have a black eye. Did nobody do that too?"

Duquesne glanced up at his daughter. "Nothing for you to worry about," he told her sternly.

Kathy shrugged one shoulder languidly. "As if I ever," she answered.

She put down the half-nibbled pastry and patted her lips with a linen napkin. Then she stood and walked away from the table.

"Where you goin'?" Duquesne asked.

Kathy shrugged again. "Nowhere!"

Duquesne looked over at the bodyguards. He jerked his head, indicating that they should accompany her, whatever her plan.

Wilbur and Chic groaned slightly, but began to follow after her.

Kathy turned, pouting with annoyance. "Oh, honestly, Daddy, do they *have* to come?"

"Just for the next couple of days," Duquesne assured her. "I'm having trouble with some people. I don't want you to have any . . . problems."

Suddenly, Kathy's pout became something darker. "Problems," she repeated. "You mean, like the kind of problems Mama had?"

Duquesne felt his blood pressure rising. He returned her look, and his voice was cold and hard. "As long as you live under my roof, in my town, you do what I say!"

Kathy stared at him for a long instant, as angry as he was. There was so much she wanted to say, she thought. And right now she dared not utter a word of it.

She shrugged, pulled her car keys from her purse, and tossed them to Wilbur.

"Fetch!" she told him. "I'm going shopping. We leave in fifteen minutes."

Then she turned and sauntered toward the door that led into the foyer.

A sleek red convertible pulled from the underground parking garage of Duquesne's building. Two goons—blond and dark—both of whom Batman had faced the night before, were in the front seat.

The blond, muscle-bound giant was driving.

In the backseat, Kathy Duquesne sat, apparently enjoying the wind in her spiky, cropped hair.

The convertible cruised smoothly past Bruce Wayne's town car, which was parked discreetly across the street from Duquesne's building.

Bruce leaned forward, speaking to Alfred, who was seated behind the wheel.

"That's her," Bruce said.

Alfred glanced in the rearview mirror at his passenger. "If I might ask . . . exactly what is it you hope to discover?"

Bruce smiled and raised an eyebrow. "What a beautiful young woman does in her free time," he said.

Alfred nodded, and his mouth twitched in an answering smile. "A pleasure drive, then," he said.

The town car pulled away from the curb.

It followed the convertible onto the freeway, then took the exit that led to the ritzy Gotham Heights neighborhood.

Gotham Heights was the toniest shopping district in the city. Its streets were lined with exclusive, chic small boutiques and trendy restaurants. It also boasted the city's most fashionable department store—Cameron's of Gotham. The city's rich and famous shopped here, and the nearby streets were lined with their limos, luxury sports vehicles, and town cars.

The red convertible lucked into a parking space in front of Cameron's. Alfred double-parked the town car several spaces behind.

As Bruce watched, the bodyguards climbed from the front seat and opened the rear passenger door.

With the goons following like lapdogs, Kathy, dressed in a clinging sundress, sashayed across the street toward a glittering shop specializing in evening wear.

Alfred pulled out the *Gotham Times* newspaper and began to peruse the front page.

Hours later, Bruce was still sitting in the backseat of the town car. He had watched as Kathy, followed closely by her increasingly laden bodyguards, strolled down one side of High Street, then up the other side, stopping in various shops.

"It appears, sir, that the young woman is doing her part to keep the American economy afloat," Alfred commented as Kathy finally pushed through the revolving door into Cameron's, followed by her long-suffering bodyguards.

Bruce drummed his fingers on the leather armrest, then stretched his legs restlessly. Seated like this in the back of the town car, he was learning nothing. He was also thoroughly bored.

By now, Alfred had the newspaper turned to the comics section. "Humph!" he said. "I see where the modern world has defeated Ziggy once again."

Bruce sighed. "Now she's in Cameron's. How many stores does this make so far?"

Alfred rolled his eyes. "Including the nail boutique? Seven." He put down the funnies and reached for the sports section. "And not one sale on explosives."

Decisively, Bruce opened the car door. "You know, Alfred, I think I could use a new watch."

Alfred didn't look up from the baseball news. "You deserve it, sir," he murmured.

Bruce strode eagerly into Cameron's plush interior, following in the wake of Kathy Duquesne.

13

Bruce walked past hats, makeup, and jewelry. No Kathy Duquesne.

He checked a directory for women's clothes, then took the escalator to the third floor.

Kathy and her entourage were in the evening wear department. The blond goon, Wilbur, was holding several dresses on hangers. Chic was balancing several hatboxes.

Kathy stood before an oval mirror, holding two more dresses, one in each hand.

She held the first in front of her, a strapless red sheath shimmering with beads, and made an approving noise in the back of her throat.

Then she held up the other—a full-skirted confection— and cringed.

"Brown taffeta. What are they thinking?" she asked.

"Put this one back too," she said, tossing it toward Wilbur. It landed, half covering his head.

Bruce stood before a jewelry display, but one eye was on Kathy. He suspected that her mindless act was exactly that.

Not that the bodyguards have a clue, Bruce thought. It

would never occur to those brutes that she was simply jerking their chains. They obviously thought her inane chatter was for real.

Bruce almost felt sorry for them. He wondered what Kathy Duquesne was really up to.

Kathy headed for the dressing room with the red beaded dress. Chic followed close on her heels.

At the dressing room entrance, she turned to face him. "It's a *women's* dressing room, Chic," she said in a patronizing voice. "You can't come in here. The worst that can happen is that I'll need a size eight. Why don't you go rob Gift Wrap or something?"

She turned on her heels and marched inside.

Bruce watched the bodyguards in the reflection of a store-counter mirror.

Chic meandered over to Wilbur, who was obediently re-hanging the rejected dresses.

"Never thought I'd say this, but I miss workin' for the Joker," Wilbur said.

Suddenly, behind him, Bruce heard Kathy's distinctive voice whisper, "Sir, could you help me?"

Bruce turned to face her. "Sorry, I don't work here," he said.

Kathy was hiding behind a pillar near the counter.

"No, not that," she whispered. "See those two men?" She pointed to Chic and Wilbur and wrinkled her nose engagingly. "I'd rather they not see me. If you could just help me get to the escalator . . ."

Whatever Bruce had been expecting to happen, this wasn't it.

"O-kay," he said hesitantly. He tried to look like a poor dupe dazzled by her beauty and eager to aid a lady in distress.

Bruce extended his arm, and she took it. They began to walk away. He kept his body between Kathy and the bodyguards, trying to screen her from their sight.

He smiled innocently. "Usually you only see things like this in the movies."

He glanced back. Wilbur had put on an outrageous pair of pink-framed ladies' sunglasses and was doing a fashion-model pose. Chic was laughing . . . until he looked past Wilbur and spotted the couple stepping onto the escalator.

"Hey!" he shouted, snatching up his pile of hatboxes and bolting after them. Wilbur grabbed his shopping bags and raced after his partner, still wearing the pink sunglasses.

Bruce and Kathy began to run down the escalator. The bodyguards pounded after them.

"Wait! Ms. Duquesne!" Chic shouted.

Kathy and Bruce darted past a Japanese tour group, which blocked Chic and Wilbur's progress.

Wilbur craned his neck, trying to peer past the sightseers. "Hey, where's she goin'?" he mumbled.

The heavily laden bodyguards shoved through the tourists and stumbled down the escalator, just as Kathy and Bruce stepped off onto the ground level.

As they leapt from the bottom step, Bruce reached down and pushed the emergency stop button.

The escalator halted abruptly. The bodyguards lost their balance and fell forward, dropping the shopping bags and hatboxes, which rolled and tumbled down the escalator steps.

Kathy looked back and grinned at the ensuing chaos. "Very inventive," she said. "You're more ingenious than you look!"

She grabbed Bruce's hand and, laughing, dragged him down a crowded aisle, but they were impeded by the crowd rushing to gawk at the escalator confusion.

Bruce glanced backward. "Keep going!" he said. "Whoever they are, they're on their feet! They're right behind us!"

"No problem!" Kathy said. "There's the door! We're almost outside."

Bruce snatched an umbrella from a display rack.

As they speeded outside through the revolving door, Bruce hooked the handle of the umbrella on the aperture's edge.

Wilbur and Chic, having abandoned their packages, rushed into the revolving door, pushing hard to hurry it along. Abruptly, the door slammed to a halt. The harder the body-guards pushed, the more tightly jammed the umbrella became.

For the moment, the door was immobilized with Chic and Wilbur effectively trapped between thick panes of glass.

"Brilliant!" Kathy said. "Just brilliant!"

She laughed up into Bruce's eyes, practically clapping her hands at the childish trick they had just played on the pursuing goons.

Bruce couldn't help grinning back.

Kathy glanced toward the door. "Some party-poop manager is busting them loose," she said. "Come on!"

She raced toward the red convertible, yanked open the driver-side door, climbed behind the wheel, and slapped on her seat belt.

She turned to Bruce, her dark eyes dancing with mischief.

"Hurry. Get in!" she said. "Unless you want that handsome face rearranged."

Bruce hopped over the door, sank into the passenger-side bucket seat, and grabbed for his seat belt.

Kathy revved the car's engine and shifted gears, and the convertible lurched away from the curb. As the bodyguards dashed from the door, the convertible peeled into traffic. The goons stared after it, fury etched clearly on their faces.

Alfred, seated behind the steering wheel of the town car,

looked up from the business section of the paper and murmured, "Oh, dear."

He thrust the town car into gear and rushed to follow, almost sideswiping the angry bodyguards as they stumbled into traffic, trying to keep their charge in sight.

14

Kathy drove quickly, handling the convertible with skill and verve. With the wind whipping her spiky hair, Bruce thought she looked not like escaped quarry, but like a wild goddess of the hunt.

"Who were they?" he finally asked.

Kathy shrugged, not taking her eyes off the road. "Daddy's bodyguards. Mine too, up till a few minutes ago."

She glanced at him, mouth tilted in an engaging grin. "You've just run off with a very notorious woman. I'm Kathy Duquesne."

When Bruce feigned a blank look, she explained, "Daughter of Carleton Duquesne?"

Bruce raised his eyebrows. "The gangster?" he asked.

Kathy turned onto the entrance ramp of the Gotham Gate Bridge, taking a corner too fast, even for Bruce.

"Yes," she said in a light, amused tone. "But we try not to use the 'G' word in front of Daddy."

She's trying to act unconcerned, Bruce thought, *but that burst of recklessness gave her away. Her father's occupation bothers her.*

The convertible roared onto the bay-spanning suspension bridge. Kathy glanced in the rearview mirror.

"This is interesting," she said. "I think we're being followed."

Bruce glanced over his shoulder. His dark town car was pulling into the lane behind them.

"Doesn't look like one of Dad's goon squad," Kathy said. She thrust out her chin. "Whoever they are, they won't be tailing us long!"

She switched gears and gunned the engine. "Hope you aren't expected anywhere," she said.

The convertible zipped forward, pulled left into an opening in traffic, then cut right again into the fast lane, leaving the larger, more ponderous town car in the dust.

Alfred slowed the sedan to a more leisurely pace and sighed. "You're on your own, Master Bruce," he said.

Bruce Wayne certainly didn't look as if he were suffering, Alfred thought. If he knew his friend, Bruce was enjoying the encounter.

Alfred sighed. *A beautiful woman, a red convertible, a sunny day. What's not to enjoy?* he asked himself. *Perhaps I'd best go home,* he thought, *and await further instructions there.*

As they approached the tollbooth at the end of the bridge, Kathy had the convertible doing near ninety. A truck had just pulled through the gate, and the jointed tollbooth arm was just coming down, roughly paralleling the road.

Bruce tensed. Kathy wasn't slowing down. He watched her lean into the wheel, clearly determined.

The convertible sped through the toll station, the top of the front windshield just nicking the descending bar, which rattled behind them.

The convertible zigzagged around the slower trucks and

sedans as it turned onto the parkway, heading away from Gotham City toward the countryside beyond.

Grinning, Kathy glanced over at Bruce and asked, "Are we having fun yet?"

Bruce and Kathy strolled along the edge of a cliff that overlooked the Atlantic. The sun, setting on the land side, threw the purple shadow of the cliff onto the rocky beach below and the sea beyond.

The air was warm and mild, soft with moisture. It mingled smells of the ocean and the meadow that lay to their left. The breaking waves slapped rhythmically below, and gulls swooped and cried overhead.

Kathy was barefoot, dangling her costly Italian-made shoes as if they were of no more value than plastic flip-flops. The hem of her sundress waved jauntily in the light, warm breeze. And she was laughing.

"Bruce Wayne." She chortled at the thought. "What a photo op. The most respected man in Gotham with the daughter of the most disrespected."

Bruce frowned. "In this town, your father has a lot of competition for that title," he said judiciously.

For some reason, this sent Kathy into another gale of laughter. "I know. Most of them come to dinner from time to time."

Slowly she sobered, the laughter in her eyes replaced by wistfulness. "I used to wonder what it would be like to come from a 'respectable' family, where there's no violence, no vendettas—no victims. What that must feel like . . ."

"I wish I could tell you," Bruce murmured.

With another of her mercurial mood changes, Kathy stood on tiptoe and twirled on the cliff's edge, flinging her arms wide as if she could fly. "It must feel like freedom!" she cried.

Bruce reached for her. "Kathy—not so near the edge," he said.

She turned to him, her mood nostalgic now. "You sound like my mother. 'Not so close, Kathy. Don't go scaring me, girl.'" She sighed.

They stopped beneath a gnarled and twisted old oak that spread its leaves above them. Kathy leaned against its rough bark, looking melancholy.

"When I was little, this was my mom's and my favorite spot. We used to come out here to paint. She was a great artist. She said I had the eye. She said, 'Honey, you could be another Carrie Mae Weems.'"

Kathy looked out at the ocean, somber now, and reflective. "Mama married my dad, not knowing what he did," Kathy said. "He . . . he lied to her, tricked her into it. By the time she found out, I had been born. She hated it, what he did. But, in spite of everything, she loved him. She'd never have left him, no matter what. . . ."

"What happened to her?" Bruce asked.

"What happened?" she whispered. "She . . . died. Isn't that what always happens?"

Always? Bruce wondered at her choice of the word. She sounded bitter. The pain of her mother's death—and her father's betrayal of her mother's trust—was still fresh for her. *However her mother's death happened, it was traumatic,* Bruce thought. *And Kathy never got over it.*

Bruce understood, better than most, the effect of childhood trauma. The memory of one triggering event was always with him.

The masked mugger, with his pistol pointing at Bruce's parents. The demand for money. The gunshots, one after the other. His parents crumpling . . . falling.

If it hadn't been for Alfred, young Bruce would have been

58

completely alone. And maybe would have gone completely mad.

Dealing with the consequences of that shock had inspired Bruce to become the man he was.

"Bruce?" Kathy asked, sounding worried.

Bruce blinked and sighed. "I was just...thinking. About your mom...I'm sorry," he murmured.

They turned in the deepening dusk and began to walk back toward the red convertible parked in a pull-over beside the road.

"Everyone's sorry," Kathy said ruefully. "It doesn't make any difference."

"How did she—" Bruce started to ask. But the rumble of a car engine interrupted his question.

"I can't believe they actually found me," Kathy murmured as a dark sedan pulled in behind the red convertible. "Wilbur and Chic are a constant source of amazement."

The long-suffering bodyguards climbed out wearily and trudged toward Bruce and Kathy, looking less than eager to reclaim their recalcitrant charge.

Kathy sighed, pulled the keys to her convertible from her pocket, and handed them to Bruce.

"Here," she said. "Bring it back sometime. Or not, if you want to keep it. There are plenty more cars where that came from."

She kissed Bruce on the cheek and trotted ahead to meet the angry bodyguards, noting their clenched fists and furious glances in Bruce Wayne's direction.

"Down, boys!" she commanded. "I kidnapped the man, not vice versa. Time to be getting home!"

She sauntered ahead of them toward the black sedan. Obediently, they followed her.

She stopped and waited while Wilbur opened the back passenger door. Then she slipped into the dark leather interior.

The goons climbed into the front seat, and Chic revved the engine.

Bruce stood on the cliff edge, watching, eyes narrowed, as the headlights of the sedan swept over him. The sedan made a U-turn. Then, with a growl of its engine, it vanished into the dusk, leaving Bruce alone with the roaring surf and wheeling gulls.

And his reluctant thoughts about Kathy Duquesne. *How did her mother die?* he wondered. He would have to find out.

15

The midnight encounter later that night at Gotham City Park wasn't formally scheduled. There had been no Bat-Signal to call a meeting.

Drug dealers had been using the area around the park's carousel as an after-hours drug mart. Several city gangs were involved in both buying and selling; there were the inevitable territorial disputes, and corpses had begun to turn up regularly. Inevitably, Gotham's finest had become involved.

Harvey Bullock and Sonia Alcana were working as part of a Gotham Police stakeout team, and Commissioner Gordon had dropped by to observe the operation.

The police were crouched among carved wooden fantasy creatures that made up the merry-go-round. Indeed, the carousel with its bizarrely shaped mythological animals was a near-perfect hiding place.

Crouched behind a prancing Pegasus, Sonia Alcana whispered, "Somebody must've tipped them. I don't think they're going to show."

"Like you're some kind of fortune-teller now?" Bullock

grumbled in a voice as rumpled as his suit as he knelt beneath a rearing dragon.

"You may be right," Commissioner Gordon murmured simultaneously, leaning against the back of a unicorn.

Despite the apparent no-shows, the three police officers remained hidden and alert for danger. All jumped when a voice behind them said, "I met Batwoman."

They didn't need to see the speaker to know who that voice belonged to.

"Batman!" Sonia whispered.

"Batwoman confirmed that the weapons we recovered were being made at the Penguin's Bric-A-Bracs factory," Batman continued.

They turned, and Batman stepped forward. His horn-headed silhouette seemed at one with the fabulous bestiary.

"Who is she?" Commissioner Gordon asked. "Who's Batwoman?"

For a moment, Batman hesitated. "I think she's Carleton Duquesne's daughter. Remember the assassination attempt on him ten years ago?"

Gordon frowned, remembering. "Yeah, the gunman missed him, hit his wife instead. Duquesne went crazy, got the goon who killed his wife, and nearly started a gang war in the process."

Batman nodded. "Kathy Duquesne was standing beside her mother, saw the bullet hit her, knelt beside her as she died. I think she blames her father for that death, and a lot more besides."

Bullock snorted. "And so she became Batwoman to try and destroy him? C'mon, she'd be bitin' the hand that feeds her! Think of the dough her old man has."

Alcana shook her head. "You can't buy peace of mind, Bullock."

Gordon glanced at Bullock and Alcana and nodded decisively. "All right, let's keep a tail on Kathy Duquesne," he said.

He turned back toward Batman to thank him, but Batman was no longer there.

Bullock groaned. "I hate it when he pulls that spooky stuff," he said.

Below the house and grounds of Wayne Manor lay a vast and secret network of caves with hidden openings onto land, sea, and air.

As a boy, Bruce Wayne had discovered the subterranean passages. But Batman had made them his own. Using the resources of the Wayne fortune, he had built a stairway that connected the caves directly to Wayne Manor, and he had converted the underground chambers to fit his own vigilante purposes.

The caves had become a gymnasium in which he honed his body; a forensic laboratory, filled with the most sensitive investigative equipment available; a high-tech computer research system to rival that of the FBI; a garage that housed various and sundry vehicles; and a museum, housing memorabilia from a hundred encounters with the cream of Gotham City's criminal masterminds.

Batman had flung aside his cape and cowl. He sat in a thronelike chair before a computer workstation, staring into a monitor.

On the screen flashed a series of images: Kathy Duquesne playing tennis, face determined, her short white tennis skirt flipping jauntily as she made a difficult shot; Kathy playing polo, riding a horse at breakneck speed, her mallet caught in mid-swing; Kathy winning a marathon, arms flung out to embrace victory as she broke the ribbon at the finish line. Her smile—confident, victorious—was enchantment itself.

Those images showed a far different woman from the vapid creature who wasted her days on shopping expeditions, he thought.

Or from the despondent daughter longing for her dead mother. Or the mischievous creature laughingly outwitting her bodyguards.

Who is Kathy Duquesne really? Batman asked himself. *Why does her involvement in this Batwoman business make me feel so sad?*

Alfred stopped beside the computer station and picked up the discarded cape.

"I see Ms. Duquesne is gifted in other sports besides extreme shopping," he said. "This bodes well for your suspicions, does it not, Master Bruce?"

Bruce rubbed his face tiredly and sighed. "I guess so, Alfred," he said.

Carrying the cape, Alfred crossed the Batcave and strolled toward the gymnasium area, where Tim Drake, in his red, black, and gold Robin costume, was hurling Batarangs at a target with a bat-shaped center.

As Alfred passed, Tim nodded toward Bruce. "What's with him?" Tim asked.

Alfred sighed. "I think he has some affection for this one," he said.

Tim shook his head, and Alfred heard him mutter, "Here we go again! Man, he sure can pick 'em."

16

Batwoman leapt from her Batglider onto the head of a fifteen-foot-high stone penguin. She tried not to notice the twenty-story drop to the ground. Because, right now, the Roost was where she needed to be.

The Roost was the name of the Dark Deco high-rise apartment building owned by the Penguin. As a monument to himself, and because it amused him, he had placed stone carvings of penguins on the facade, where an ordinary building might have displayed common, everyday gargoyles.

I doubt he realized how much easier the statues make it to perch here, she thought. *Or to break into his apartment.*

Balancing carefully, she leapt from the stone penguin's head onto a narrow ledge, then sidled to the right until she was standing before a darkened window.

Yep, she noted. *Even up here, it's locked. Luckily, I came prepared.*

She withdrew a rectangular device from her pouch and held it up to the old-fashioned window sash. The lock snapped open. She waited, but no alarm sounded.

It worked, she thought triumphantly. *I'm in!*

Or maybe not. She tugged at the window sash, trying to lift it, but it wouldn't budge.

"Darn!" she grumbled. "The blasted thing's been painted shut."

She lifted again, putting all her considerable strength behind the movement. With a sudden lurch, the window jerked open. Overbalanced and surprised, Batwoman almost toppled from the ledge.

She grasped the sash with trembling fingers. Then, oh so carefully, she braced herself and slipped inside.

As she had planned, she entered the Penguin's home office. She switched on a narrow-beamed penlight, then glanced around.

The room was small, maybe ten feet square. There was a desk and chair, with its back to the window. Unfortunately, the desk held no computer, which meant she would have to search for hard copy. On the left wall was a row of file cabinets. Across from them, on the right wall, was a closed door.

Except for the abundance of penguin paraphernalia, there was nothing special about the room. No clue telling Batwoman where exactly she should look for the data she needed.

She tried the desk drawers first, opening them one by one and rifling through them quickly. Expertly.

Nothing, she thought. *Better check the file cabinets next. But where do I begin?*

Stealthily, she slipped across the floor, cautious not to make a sound.

She checked the labels on the cabinets. Then, breathing a prayer for silence, she pulled open a file drawer. It squeaked almost inaudibly.

Nothing to worry about, she reassured herself. Her research had shown that at this time of night the Penguin was always at his nightclub. A little squeak hardly mattered.

She froze as a cultured voice hissed angrily from the room beyond, "I don't think you appreciate the precariousness of our perch, Thorne, especially now that we have no factory."

Guessed wrong on that one, she thought. The Penguin was back. And Rupert Thorne was with him. She'd better find what she needed and get out fast.

In the adjacent den, the Penguin gestured for his guest to be seated, then settled back in a wingback chair.

"If we're unable to deliver the rest of our stockpile, we're dead, Thorne." The dapper little man waved his umbrella irritably as he continued his diatribe. "The Kaznians will come after us like slathering carnivores. We'll be begging for prison."

Thorne threw himself into a sturdy leather easy chair. "Duquesne says he can handle the bat broad," he said. He pulled out his deck of cards and began his nervous one-handed shuffle.

"She almost killed Batman, for heaven's sake!" the Penguin squeaked, stabbing the air with his umbrella for emphasis. "Normally, I would find that commendable, but now it just proves that Duquesne is out of his league. We need some real muscle."

The Penguin stopped his diatribe and stared intently at the crack at the bottom of the door that led into his office. He was almost certain he had caught a faint flash of light.

Signaling Thorne to move up behind him, the Penguin rose silently and crept to the door.

Slowly, soundlessly, he edged it open and looked inside.

Batwoman was standing in his office, before the file cabinet. Her back was to him, and she was taking photos of a file propped on an open drawer. The light he had seen came from the flash of her subminiature camera.

Before the Penguin could aim his umbrella, Batwoman whirled, held up the camera, and flashed it over and over, right in the small man's eyes.

The Penguin raised his umbrella, pointed it in her direction, and fired blindly. The tip of the umbrella ejected and whizzed past Batwoman, missing her by inches. It blasted into the open file cabinet, blowing it apart.

Batwoman spun and kicked out at the door, which slammed closed, knocking the Penguin back toward the den. The little man smacked into Thorne, who toppled into a lamp and small table, overturning both amid a shower of playing cards.

The Penguin and Thorne struggled to their feet, shoved open the door, and stumbled into the dark office.

"There she is!" Thorne shouted. "At the window!"

Batwoman crouched on the sill. As the Penguin raised his umbrella and fired, she leapt out the open window. The missile hurtled past her.

The Penguin and Thorne dashed over and looked outside. Batwoman had landed on her Batglider. She was already zooming out of range.

They jerked backward as the missile exploded, demolishing the stone head of one of the building's decorative penguins.

"That does it, Penguin," Thorne growled, his voice low and mean. "Whoever you want to bring in to deal with this witch is fine with me!"

17

Kathy Duquesne stepped from her rooftop swimming pool and reached for a towel. She always felt more peaceful after an hour of exercise, and serenity was a quality she valued greatly.

Her sense of well-being was shattered by the loud crash coming from her father's office. She snatched up the towel and looked around. For once, no one was watching her. *Good!*

Kathy crept toward the half-open French door that led to her father's office. Listening through the crack, she heard her father growl unintelligibly.

She peeked through the paned window. Her father was sweeping his arm across his desk, sending everything on it—phone, laptop, papers—flying to the floor. She had never seen him in such a rage, not even when her mother was killed in his stead.

Chic was cringing, his back to the French door. "Who're they g-getting, boss?" Kathy heard Chic stammer. "Who's better than you?"

Duquesne growled, "Penguin's not sayin'!"

Then he looked up, suddenly conscious that Chic was in the

room witnessing his humiliation and loss of control. Duquesne turned on Chic and snarled, "Get out! Get out!"

Bowing, practically groveling, Chic rushed for the door that led to the foyer.

Outside the French door, Kathy leaned against the wall of the penthouse and smiled. *Welcome to reality, Daddy dear!* she thought fiercely. *Mom begged you to cut your ties with these creeps. But no! Not you! Even after she died, you kept associating with them. Gave them your loyalty.*

But present them with one tiny problem and let's see how fast they turn on you. They're losers . . . and you'll lose by association; that I promise you!

The science lab of WayneTech was lit by floor-to-ceiling windows offering a panoramic view of the Gotham City skyline. But Dr. Rocky Ballentine was unaware of the glorious sunset right outside her window. Her entire attention was focused on a computer-screen image of a stone hallway and an ornately carved arched wooden door set in a jewel-studded portal.

"First you click on the red crystal," she said.

She moved the cursor to the left and clicked on an irregular jewel-like stone set above a door.

"Then the blue . . . ," she continued as she clicked on a blue jewel set in the handle. "Then you hold down the shift key."

Suddenly, the music changed, the door opened, and on the computer screen, a crystal-studded cavern filled with treasure appeared.

"Whoa! You got in!" Tim Drake shouted enthusiastically. "Excellent!"

Smiling modestly, Rocky popped out the game disc and handed it back to Tim. "I've raided a few tombs in my time."

"Tim, you're not bothering Rocky again, are you?" Bruce Wayne asked.

Tim and Rocky turned to face him as he stepped into the office. Both looked guilty.

"Get off our case, Bruce, it's way after five!" Tim began defensively.

Then Tim grinned. "She found the secret bonus level to Death Castle 3000! Nobody at school can figure it out, not even Deek 'the Geek' Berkowitz. He's gonna flip!"

"So is Alfred," Bruce answered. "He's been waiting in the car for you all this time."

The guilty look had returned to Tim's face. "Ewww . . . I forgot. Sorry."

Tim turned to Rocky. "Gotta run," he said. "Thanks." Holding his game disc, he dashed down the hall that led to the elevators.

Bruce smiled at Rocky. "Working late again?" he asked.

Rocky smiled ruefully. "Yeah. Fortunately, my boyfriend is very understanding. What about yours?"

Bruce raised an eyebrow.

"Um . . . I mean girlfriend." Rocky flushed, suddenly embarrassed. "I mean, of course, girlfriend; after all, considering your reputation . . . not that it's bad or anything, or even any of my business 'cause it's not . . ."

She paused, took a deep breath, then asked, "I was just curious—how red is my face?"

"Crimson," Bruce said, grinning at her monologue. He took a seat on the corner of her desk. She looked very pretty with her pink cheeks and her blond, flyaway curls. "And no, I don't have anybody special."

"Am I that forgettable, Bruce?" a sultry voice asked from the doorway.

Bruce and Rocky turned.

Kathy Duquesne was drop-dead gorgeous and she knew it. She was dressed in a slinky red strapless knee-length sheath. Around her neck was a diamond choker. Red gloves rose above her elbows, and her stiletto heels matched the bright color of her dress.

Her heels clicked like muted gunshots as she walked toward Bruce.

"I've managed to lose my shadows for a little while, so I thought I'd paint the town red," she whispered seductively, stroking a bloodred fingertip gently down his cheek. "Want to come along and empty a few spray cans?"

Bruce found her smile nearly irresistible. For a moment, he stood there, grinning like an idiot.

Then he saw Rocky, still sitting at her computer, gawking up at them both. Belatedly remembering his manners, he introduced the two women. "Excuse me—Kathy Duquesne, Roxanne Ballentine."

Smiling, Kathy turned to Rocky, hand extended. "Pleased to meet you!" she said.

Completely flustered, Rocky popped up like toast from a toaster and shook the proffered hand a bit too vigorously.

"Yes. I'm sorry," Rocky blurted out.

Confused, Kathy asked, "About what?"

Rocky blinked, then looked as if she wanted to sink through the floor. Blushing even redder, she stammered, "I-I don't know!"

18

Bruce Wayne stood on the balcony above the sweeping double escalators and looked down at the sunken main floor of the Iceberg Lounge with a jaundiced eye. But even he had to admit that the decor looked spectacular.

As he rode down the moving stairway, Bruce studied the interior.

The main floor, where the nightclub patrons danced and dined, was below street level. The room was vast and circular, with a ring of brass-railed balconies, held up by judiciously placed pillars, overhanging the main floor. The balconies created a dropped ceiling over part of the dining area and gave some tables the illusion of privacy, even intimacy.

And since it was named the Iceberg Lounge, it would, of course, have a polar theme.

A hostess in a tight, strapless leotard, wearing a bow tie and bowler hat, led them past marble columns and candlelit tables.

As she led Kathy Duquesne and Bruce Wayne past the tables, several guests smiled at Kathy or called out greetings.

"Hey, Kaytee!" a mustached gangster type shouted.

A wise guy pulled off his dark glasses for a closer look, then clicked his tongue admiringly. "Lookin' hot!"

"Got some fries wit' that shake?" a goon with a crooked nose asked riotously.

Kathy returned their greetings with a sultry smile, a waggle of her fingers, and a raised eyebrow.

But Bruce just frowned. Clearly, Kathy was comfortable in this environment. He was not.

The hostess led them toward a table beside a half-moon, water-filled pool where live seals frolicked in the water.

Just ahead, a half circle–shaped stage was cantilevered twelve feet above the dance floor. Before the stage, a glittering, mountainous, pseudo-iceberg rose. Atop the iceberg, a torch singer was standing, belting out a song with a hot Latin beat and lyrics of love and loss.

Around the iceberg, and below the stage, the dancers were shaking their booties.

As they sat, Kathy noticed Bruce's critical expression.

"I know," she said, bristling defensively. "Not exactly the book club crowd."

Still scowling, Bruce said, "I assume you know who owns this place."

As if on cue, the Penguin stepped up to their table. Ever the gracious host, he took Kathy's hand, but his malicious eyes were fastened on Bruce.

"She *should* know whose club this is," the Penguin said. "I bought Kathy her first parasol."

Bending over her hand, the Penguin kissed it graciously. "Kathleen," he said.

"Ozzie," Kathy replied, dimpling engagingly.

The Penguin extended his hand to Bruce. "And Mr. Wayne. It's been quite a while, hasn't it?"

"Yes," Bruce sneered, sitting stiff and unmoving, disdaining the proffered welcome. "I believe the last time was when you stole plutonium from one of my labs and threatened to blow up the city."

"Oh. Oh yes!" The Penguin chortled gleefully, as if remembering an old and harmless prank. "Back in my more rambunctious days . . ."

Another hostess in a bowler hat stepped up to the Penguin and whispered, "Excuse me, sir. But your call just came in."

The Penguin sighed and stepped back, away from their table. "Ah, the vagaries of a restaurateur. You understand." The dapper little man doffed his hat and disappeared into the crowd.

Bruce glowered after him.

Kathy sighed. "I didn't know you and the Penguin had issues."

Bruce crossed his arms across his chest. "It's not that popinjay that's bothering me. It's you. What kind of game are you playing?"

Kathy opened her eyes wide. "Game?" she asked.

Bruce waved his hand, encompassing the club and its patrons. "You dump your bodyguards for a private night out and where do you choose to go?" he asked. "A club where half the patrons are your father's cronies. It's like you want him to hear about this.

"So I ask myself, Why?" he continued. "I figure you must be trying to prove something, to make some point. To send a message. Otherwise, it doesn't make sense."

Expression frozen, Kathy stood abruptly. "I'm not sure I like your tone," she said coldly. "I'll visit the powder room and decide there."

Strutting away from their table, she trilled, "Ta-ta," and wiggled her fingers.

There was another message in that dismissive leave-taking, Bruce thought, scowling after her. He wondered if Kathy would be coming back.

19

The Penguin entered his shadowed, mahogany-paneled upstairs office and shut the door quietly.

He settled into his plush leather, wheeled desk chair, removed his signature top hat, and placed his umbrella to one side of the blotter. A lone lamp spot-lit his massive table-style desk.

The Penguin smiled. *The room is a visual metaphor for my own contradictory psyche,* he thought. *I am a man who craves the spotlight, but operates in the shadows.*

Relaxed and comfortable, finally, he picked up his cell phone.

"So you've already landed," he said. "Splendid! How soon before we can convene?"

More darkness. Deeper shadows.

The large man sitting in the back of the limousine preferred them. In fact, he insisted on them; he was most comfortable in the shadow world of intrigue.

He was a trained killer and a brilliant military strategist

from South America who had been transformed into an unstoppable super-soldier during an experimental operation that implanted tubes into his brain. Through these tubes he could inject a steroidlike chemical called Venom directly into his system, augmenting his body mass and strength, at will.

His name was Bane, and he had been hired by the Penguin to become Batwoman's worst nightmare.

Only his glittering dark eyes and mouth were visible through the black mask that covered his entire head.

"I can drop by your club tonight," Bane said. In contrast to his hulking, brutish body, his voice was cultured and musical, with a faint Castilian accent. "I assume you have a back entrance."

"Oh yes!" Penguin said. Bane's voice, so refined and melodious, so cold, gave even the Penguin a chill. He rushed out his answer, joking and anxious to hide his momentary unease. "I use it so much I'm thinking of installing a revolving door. See you then."

The Penguin set down the phone.

With great satisfaction he glanced around his office, the heart of his domain, and realized, with a sinking feeling, that he was not alone.

He squinted past the lamp at the shadowy figure standing beside the door and snapped, "I said I wasn't to be disturbed!"

"Oh, am I disturbing you?" asked a sultry female voice. "Can't have that, can we?" She stepped into the spotlight.

"Batwoman!" the Penguin cried. He grabbed for his umbrella, but Batwoman reached it first. She pulled a metal ball from a belt pouch and tossed it at him.

The blob hit the Penguin in the chest, then, instantly, began to shape-shift, sending wirelike cables snaking up and around him, binding his arms to his body, and his body to his chair. He struggled, but couldn't break free.

Batwoman stepped forward, hooked the vest-front of the bound Penguin with the handle of the umbrella, and jerked him forward, so that the desk cut into his belly.

"How dare you?" the Penguin shouted. "Release me at once, you harridan, or I'll—" Abruptly, he stopped talking. His bonds were getting tighter, making groves in the back of his leather chair. Cutting groves in him.

"These things are constricting!" he gasped.

The Penguin could see the ghost of a smile behind Batwoman's gauzy mask.

"That's right, fat boy," Batwoman whispered. "They'll slice you like the cheese you are, unless you tell me who your new player is."

The Penguin scowled mutinously and struggled to break free. Nobody talked to him like that and lived.

Trying to ignore the pain from his tightening bonds, he felt below the edge of the desk and depressed a panic button.

Seated at his table beside the seal pool, Bruce Wayne watched as two of the bowler-hatted hostesses began to move with grim determination past him toward a service door. Beyond it, Bruce knew, lay a hidden staircase that led to the Penguin's private upstairs office.

The focused intensity of the women's movements made it obvious to Bruce that, despite their fanciful consumes, they were hired muscle, and there was trouble brewing.

Bruce looked around. Kathy was nowhere in sight.

Kathy, whom he suspected of being Batwoman. Who clearly had it in for the Penguin.

Eyes narrowing, Bruce stood and walked smoothly toward a nearby maintenance door.

As Batman, he had made it his business to learn as much

as possible about the Penguin's known enterprises. That information was going to come in handy, and not for the first time.

Upstairs, Batwoman leaned over the hapless Penguin. "Who, Penguin?" she demanded. "Who have you hired as protection? Who's the big bad boogie man?"

The red-faced little man had finally ceased struggling against his bonds. He groaned, an unintelligible sound of impotent fury.

Batwoman bent over him and whispered, singsong, in his ear, "I can't hear youuuuu. . . ."

The Penguin spat out a single word—short, clear, and terrible: "Bane!"

Batwoman jerked back. "Bane?"

Clearly, the Penguin thought, she was shocked, even alarmed. Good! Bane would be there soon. The Penguin just had to hold on.

Have to keep breathing, he told himself. *Long enough . . . to see Bane . . . destroy her.*

With a resounding *Wham!* his office door burst open.

Bane! the Penguin thought.

Through tunneling vision, the Penguin saw not Bane, but two women in hostess costumes standing in the open portal.

His bodyguards. His own little welcome committee, the Penguin thought, almost affectionately.

Blond, bouncy Anna had kicked open the door. And darkhaired, svelte Frieda, bless her rotten little soul, was hurling a barrage of throwing stars at Batwoman's heart.

Batwoman ducked and dodged.

Three throwing stars whizzed past her, barely missing the

shorter Penguin, who was still wired to his chair. With three small thuds, the weapons embedded in the wall behind him.

Anna let out a shrill cry and lunged at Batwoman in a classic knife-hand attack.

Batwoman dodged, and the blow struck the center of the table-desk, cleaving it in half.

"You may be an amoral, self-serving creep," Batwoman stated. "But you definitely don't hire pushovers."

The other bodyguard—Frieda—leapt at Batwoman. Batwoman ducked, spun, and kicked out. Frieda went flying back, but her partner began to press the attack.

As an all-out martial arts fight raged around him, the Penguin, purple-faced and struggling to draw a breath, glanced backward. Right behind him, a throwing star was lodged about three feet up the wall.

There's a chance, the Penguin thought. *One chance to free myself before I black out. Or get caught in the crossfire.* The bound man raised a leg and kicked hard against the splintered half of the desk.

The chair rolled back and slammed into the embedded star. With a *Ping!* the constricting wires parted.

The Penguin clutched his chest, gasping for breath. His coat had been shredded by the restraining wires, but at least he was free.

Around him the pitched battle between Batwoman and his bodyguards continued. Batwoman was holding her own against the two, but was outnumbered and unable to press the attack.

Anna and Frieda leapt at Batwoman together, kicking out at her simultaneously.

Batwoman flew backward, past the Penguin, and crashed through the wall beyond his desk.

20

Batwoman found herself sprawled among the members of the band. The wall of the Penguin's second-floor office obviously backed onto the musicians' stage, cantilevered above the restaurant.

That room has major soundproofing! Batwoman thought. The Penguin's office had been quiet, but the noise within the Iceberg Lounge was near deafening. Shouts and laughter came from the dining area. The musicians were playing a pulsing melody; the singer was belting out lyrics. The raucous crowd on the dance floor was rocking to their Latin beat.

So at first, only the musicians took any notice of Batwoman's unexpected arrival.

Then two furies in hostess costumes leapt through the hole and onto the stage after her.

A side kick sent Anna crashing into, then through, the bass drum.

The abrupt scattering of musicians, the cessation of the music, the sudden relative silence caught everyone's attention.

The patrons of the club—dancers and diners alike—craned their necks toward the stage as Frieda aimed a high spin kick at Batwoman's head. Batwoman ducked and blocked the blow, then toppled the hostess onto a synthesizer.

Anna disentangled herself from the rim of the destroyed bass drum, rolled to her feet, then dove low, hitting Batwoman with a flying tackle. Batwoman and the blond hostess toppled from the stage and fell twelve feet to land on the dance floor.

Amid screams and cries of outrage, would-be dancers dodged the battling women. Diners rose from their tables and, with panicked cries, raced toward the door.

Anna and Batwoman joined in a lightning-speed karate match, making moves and blocking blows with life-or-death precision. Finally, Batwoman hurled Anna into one of the tables that rimmed the dance floor.

Batwoman was looking around for an exit when dark-haired Frieda stumbled up from beneath the shattered synthesizer. She leapt from the stage, tackling Batwoman as Batwoman turned to flee.

The blond Anna picked herself up from the smashed table. Grabbing a broken table leg in her right hand, then holding it like a bat, she raced toward the fight. But before Anna could bring the club down on Batwoman's head, Batwoman kicked out backward, slamming the bodyguard in the stomach. Anna crashed backward, and the splintered chair leg went flying.

The Penguin, coat shredded but armed with his umbrella, climbed through the hole in his office wall and rushed onto the stage.

He stood for an instant, surveying the chaos.

Batwoman and his bodyguards were a tumbling blur of movement. In the dim light, he could barely tell one woman from the other.

Then Batwoman broke free.

Perched on the edge of the stage, the Penguin raised his

umbrella and aimed down at the annoying, self-proclaimed heroine.

"A bat-seeking missile for you, my dear!" he murmured, and pressed the release button. The tip of the umbrella shot off like a miniature rocket.

Batwoman dove aside. The missile raced past her, then circled in midair and came right back at her.

"Bat-seeking missile," she muttered. "Guess that was more than a metaphor."

She hurled a Batangle with cable attached toward a chandelier. It caught, and she swung up and around, dodging the missile that turned again to follow her.

Then, right in front of a marble column, she dropped to the ground. The missile was coming straight at her.

She saw the two bodyguards positioning themselves nearby as well.

At the last second, she dodged left, dropped to the ground, and rolled. The rocket slammed into the pillar and detonated.

The sound was deafening. Both bodyguards were blown back by the blast.

Harvey Bullock and Sonia Alcana were on surveillance, parked in an unmarked car across the street from the Iceberg Lounge.

Bullock was behind the wheel, upending an empty donut carton over his open mouth, then patting the bottom of the box to avoid missing a single sugary morsel. Crumbs spattered his shirtfront like snowflakes.

Sonia rolled her eyes. "Gimme a break, Bullock," she said. "It's not like you're gonna waste away if you miss a speck!"

"Hey! Powdered sugar's my favorite!" Bullock answered. He swiped his hand across his sticky mouth.

"And your second favorite's any other flavor—" Sonia broke off abruptly as a loud blast came from the nightclub.

She sat up straighter, suddenly tense.

The front door of the Iceberg Lounge burst open, and a crowd of screaming, well-dressed men and women rushed from its graceful deco portal, across the sidewalk, and into the night.

Sonia thrust open the passenger door. "Call for backup!" she shouted, and raced toward the club entrance.

For an instant, within the Iceberg Lounge, Batwoman faced the Penguin.

"Thanks for the help, Penguin!" she shouted defiantly.

How amusingly ironic! she thought. The Penguin's concussion missiles had stunned his own bodyguards, leaving her free to escape. *If* she could evade the remainder of his missiles.

Only one way to find out, she thought, and raced for an exit.

The Penguin stood on the stage, umbrella raised, and calmly fired a second projectile.

Batwoman leapt to the side, and the missile struck the wall beside her.

Too close! she thought as the concussion blast slammed her to her hands and knees. For a minute, she crouched there, too stunned by the impact to move.

Again the Penguin aimed his umbrella right at the fallen Batwoman. "Time to clip your wings, my dear," he said.

21

For an instant, Batman crouched on the brass railing of a high balcony above the stage, getting his bearings. Down below, on the main floor, men and women were screaming as they rushed toward the escalators.

Near the seal pool, Batwoman was on her knees, stunned by the Penguin's concussion missile. The Penguin, atop the stage, had her in his sights. One more missile would finish her.

Batman fired a grapnel at a chandelier, then swung downward. As the Penguin depressed the Fire button on his umbrella shaft, Batman slammed him in the back, knocking him off the stage.

As the Penguin sailed through the air, the concussion missile fired upward toward the roof. It hit the ceiling and exploded dramatically, blowing a five-foot-wide hole that opened the club interior to the shrouded Gotham sky.

The Penguin slammed into a table beside the seal pool, which collapsed beneath his weight. He landed in an undignified sprawl on the floor. Plaster from the ruined ceiling rained down on him.

As Batman leapt from the stage toward the Penguin, two thugs charged in, weapons raised.

Before they could pull the triggers, Batman hurled several Batarangs. The blades slashed the hands of the two goons, and with yelps of pain, they dropped their guns.

Several more thugs jumped on Batman from behind. As he grappled with the goons beside the seal pool, from the corner of his eye Batman spotted the Batwoman standing at the edge of the room. She was staring up through the hole in the ceiling, punching a control on her belt. He knew what that meant.

Batman was kicking the last thug away when Batwoman's glider dropped through the opening. Still seeming a bit dazed, she stumbled onto the jet board. She crouched on it as it rose, carrying her up through the opening and out into the night.

Batman was ready to fire a grapnel at the retreating glider when he saw something that froze him in mid-action. Along with several other ladies, Kathy Duquesne, looking worried and frightened, was huddled against a wall near the powder room, where the women had been when the fight broke out.

I was so sure she was Batwoman, he thought. *Looks like I was wrong.* He didn't know whether to be glad or sorry.

Suddenly a chair shattered across the back of the distracted Batman.

Batman reeled forward and splashed into the seal pool.

The Penguin, looking bruised and tattered, clambered to his feet beside the pool. He aimed a missile at the water, waiting for Batman to surface.

"I switched to an umbrella with a machine gun tip," the little man said. Then he chortled. "Self-defense. Batman was breaking and entering. No jury in the world will convict me!"

Batman was about to surface when machine gun fire broke the water above his head. Changing his mind, he held his breath and dove for the bottom.

Though the transparent edge of the pool rose above the floor level, so the diners could watch the seals at play, the pool itself was sunk an additional eight feet below the floor level. Those walls had been painted a deep, dark indigo.

Good! Batman thought. *That will make it harder for them to spot me.*

Still holding his breath, Batman circled around the pool until he had reached the wall right below where the Penguin was standing.

He pulled a cup-sized bomb from his Utility Belt and slapped it against the side of the pool. Then he dove and swam rapidly underwater to the far side of the pool.

The Penguin stepped forward until he was almost at the pool edge and peered down toward the dark bottom, his remaining thugs flanking him.

"Come on!" the Penguin shouted. "Let's see those pointy little ears one more time!"

Suddenly, the wall of the pool in front of the Penguin exploded. Water gushed from the breach in the wall, rushing right at the Penguin and carrying several barking, clapping seals with it.

The flood broke over the Penguin, sweeping the dapper little man and his goons off their feet and covering the nearby floor in several feet of water.

* * *

Batman climbed from the pool, fighting the current. Then, arm raised, he aimed his grappling hook up toward one of the high balconies and fired.

The hook caught on a brass railing, and Batman was pulled upward. He swung toward the back of the club and disappeared into the darkness.

22

Guns drawn, Alcana and Bullock fought their way through the retreating crowd exiting the Iceberg Lounge. When they finally reached the litter-strewn interior, the chaos before them left them gawking with amazement.

The dance floor was awash in water. Seals cavorted playfully among overturned furniture. A five-foot-wide hole had been blown in the ceiling. Smoke filled the air, and debris littered every surface.

The Penguin's men were stumbling to their feet, looking dazed and battered. The Penguin himself was sitting in the midst of the soggy chaos with a seal practically in his lap. As Alcana and Bullock watched, it barked loudly and slapped the Penguin on the side of the head with its tail.

Bullock scratched his head and looked around for someone to arrest. He glanced at Sonia, who was looking equally bemused.

"Must've been one heck of a floor show," Bullock said.

In his limousine, Bane cruised slowly past the Iceberg Lounge, studying the club's deco marquee and spotlit exterior through the limo's darkened windows. Panicked-looking patrons were stumbling from the open doors, and smoke was drifting from a hole in the roof.

Through a crack in his window, Bane heard the honking noise of seals echoing from the club's interior. Police cars, sirens blaring, were beginning to arrive on the scene. He scowled and settled back against the soft leather seat.

"Keep going," he told the driver in a calm voice. "It seems apparent that the Penguin is in no condition to discuss business . . . or receive visitors."

Bruce Wayne escorted Kathy Duquesne into the lobby of her father's apartment building. She clutched Bruce's arm, their previous differences apparently forgotten.

The lobby was richly furnished and large enough to accommodate several chandeliers, but neither Bruce nor Kathy noted anything special in that. Both were used to opulent surroundings.

"I have to admit," Bruce said, "it's not every date I have that ends with a police investigation."

Kathy looked up at him. Her mouth smiled, but her eyes looked sad.

"You poor thing," she teased. "Every time we're together I seem to risk your life."

Then her mouth lost the smile, and she hung her head. "I'm sorry about tonight. You were right about me."

They stopped at the private elevator door that led to her penthouse apartment. Bruce turned her to face him.

"No, no. Don't say that," he said. "I *wasn't* right. I jumped to conclusions. I tend to be too judgmental about people. All that respectability, you know." He smiled ruefully. "It really is a curse."

He stepped close until they were almost touching. "I was wrong about you. And tonight . . . tonight was wonderful." He leaned down to kiss her.

She stood on tiptoe to meet him halfway.

Before their lips could touch, the *Ping!* of the elevator bell interrupted them. The doors slid open. Chic was waiting inside, arms crossed, an annoyed scowl on his face.

"The old man wants you," he growled.

Kathy stepped away from Bruce, the magic of the moment evaporating.

"I'd invite you in," she said with a regretful smile, "but I think it's going to be a bit chilly upstairs."

She turned on her stiletto heels and stepped into the elevator. Waving her fingers backward, she murmured, "Ta-ta."

The elevator doors swished shut behind her.

23

Detective Sonia Alcana was waiting on the deserted subway platform at the Main Street station, below Police Headquarters.

After hours spent at the Iceberg Lounge interviewing those patrons and staff that the police could snag, then more hours filling out paperwork, she was exhausted.

She smiled and shook her head, a little amazed. The Batwoman was keeping one step ahead of the cops . . . and Batman too, apparently. But this time she had barely escaped. Next time . . .

Sonia pulled a Batarang from her jacket pocket and studied it thoughtfully.

"Souvenir?" Batman's gruff, distinctive voice came from behind her. She would have known it anywhere.

She smiled and turned to face him. "I found it in the Penguin's club," she said, holding the Batarang out to him. "How about an autograph? Make it a real collectors' item."

Batman took the proffered Batarang and folded it with the ease of long habit. "What did you learn at the lounge?" he asked.

Sonia smiled crookedly. "Well, other than the fact that Kathy Duquesne can't be Batwoman, not much." As she spoke, Batman tucked the Batarang into his belt.

"The Penguin gave us a statement," she continued. "Sounds like Batwoman was shaking him down. Of course, he can't imagine why—after all, he's legit now, just an honest businessman."

Batman flipped open his belt pouch and pulled out several lumps of metal and tangled wire.

"I found these in the Penguin's office," he said. "I think Batwoman used this device to bind him."

Batman pocketed one piece and handed Sonia the other.

Sonia frowned up at him. "You know that removing evidence from the scene of a crime is . . ."

She hesitated, taking in his grim, implacable expression. *Why waste my breath?* she thought.

". . . is probably not going to lose you any sleep," she concluded.

One side of Batman's mouth tilted slightly. Her reply had obviously amused him. "Call it a souvenir," he said.

He stepped back, already beginning to meld into the darkness.

Suddenly, Sonia blurted out, "You saved my life, once."

Batman stopped and turned, looking back at her from the shadows.

"Six years ago. Arsonists . . . they burned my parents' store. I was sleeping. . . . We lived on the second floor." Sonia stared into the distance as she mentally relived the traumatic event.

"I woke up and my room was filled with smoke. I was disoriented. . . . Couldn't even find the bedroom window. The floor got hot. . . . Then, all of a sudden, flames were shooting up between the floorboards."

She turned her head, looked directly into Batman's eyes. "And then . . . there you were."

Batman nodded slowly. "I remember. The arsonists were working for Rupert Thorne—part of his protection racket. The DA could never make the case stick."

Sonia nodded, her face grim with sadness and anger, her voice bitter. "Yes. Plenty of circumstantial evidence, but no physical evidence remained that proved Thorne's goons were the ones responsible. Even though everyone knew . . ."

With wrenching effort, she snapped back to the present. "Anyway, that's why I decided to become a cop." She tried to smile. "I just . . . thought you should know."

Sonia became aware of an increasingly loud rumble and the slight vibration of the platform beneath her feet. She glanced down the track and spotted the headlight of the Uptown Express speeding along the track toward her. Then its light washed over her, banishing shadows.

Sonia turned back toward Batman . . . and realized that she was standing in the station alone.

Seated in his Batcave lab, Batman examined the piece of wire under an electron microscope. The electron probe results were displayed in a spectrum graph that filled a computer screen.

In the nearby gym area, Tim was working out, pulling himself up on gymnastic rings, then doing a handstand. Upside down, he glanced at the computer screen.

"Hey, cool colors," he said. "What's it mean?"

Batman glanced at the teenager, his expression grim. "The wire from the Penguin's office is identical to that new alloy Dr. Ballentine developed for WayneTech."

"Rocky?" Tim asked, looking shocked. He held the pose for a second longer, then let go, flipping off the rings and landing perfectly.

He grabbed a towel and wiped the sweat from his face. "You think someone's using Rocky's stuff?"

Batman frowned, obviously disturbed by this turn of events.

"I don't know what to think," he said.

24

As usual, when Roxanne Ballentine visited Gotham City's Stonegate Prison, the skies were overcast and threatening rain.

As she entered the visitors' antechamber, Rocky felt her stomach clench. *Get over it,* she told herself. *It's not like you haven't done this a hundred times already.*

She stood with legs spread and arms outstretched, trying to quell her nervousness, as a female guard ran a metal detector over her.

As always, the scan was negative. The guard told her to proceed.

She walked through a small, glassed-in vestibule called a sally port, where a bored male guard punched a button. The door opened, and Rocky stepped through into the visitors' chamber.

It was a large room, cut in half by a thick glass window. A metal table ran the length of the wall, spanning both sides of the glass. Metal folding chairs provided seating.

Several convicts dressed in prison orange were talking via phones to their friends and loved ones on the other side of the glass. There was no chance for truly private conversations. No chance to touch.

Rocky took a seat on one of the metal chairs, across from a young and handsome Asian man. His hair was close-cropped, and his eyes were sunken. He looked as if he hadn't had a good night's sleep in a long time.

Rocky felt tears well up in her eyes and quickly dashed them aside. Tears were the last thing her fiancé needed to see.

She picked up the phone. "Kevin, are you okay?" She made her voice bright and encouraging, but couldn't hide the desperate worry in her eyes.

Kevin stared back with once-bright eyes now grown cold and dim. "No, Rocky, I'm not okay. I'm so far from okay, I can't even see okay from here."

Rocky brightened her expression, determined to infuse new hope into him. "Don't give up, Kevin," she said. "We're close. Really close. Once I find someone in the Penguin's organization who's willing to talk—"

Kevin interrupted her. "Rocky, you can't keep doing this! It's too dangerous. If the Penguin finds out you're spying on him—"

He looks more worried now, Rocky thought, *but at least he looks alive.*

"He won't," she interjected, her eyes wide, her expression as firmly confident as she could make it. "Kevin, I can take care of myself. I'm not the shrinking violet I used to be." She laughed, unable to hide the slight undertone of bitterness. "I've changed. I've had to."

"Listen to me," Kevin said. "You'd have to be Supergirl to have a chance against the Penguin's goons."

His voice was gruffer now and rising in volume. He was beginning to get angry.

Let him be mad, then, Rocky told herself. *Better mad than defeated and depressed.* Heck, she was beginning to get mad too.

Rocky thrust out her chin. "You don't know what I've been doing these last four years—" she said.

Behind the window partition, Kevin held up a hand, stopping her. The stubborn thrust of his chin mirrored Rocky's.

"Look, Rocky, I . . ." He hesitated, then took the plunge. "I don't want to see you anymore."

Rocky felt her face grow hot and red. Then white as the blood left her head. For an instant, she felt as if she were going to faint.

"You—you aren't—" she stammered.

"Serious?" Kevin finished the sentence for her. "I'm dead serious. I've got five more years in this hole before I even get a shot at parole. It's stupid for you to waste your life waiting for me."

Rocky's eyes narrowed dangerously. "Maybe," she growled. "But it's my life to waste. I can spend it any way I see fit!"

Kevin stood abruptly, still holding the phone. Rocky could see he was steeling himself to do what he truly believed was right.

"Don't come again," he said into the receiver. "If you do, I'll refuse to see you!" He slammed down the phone and, without looking at her, turned and stomped to the door.

Rocky jumped to her feet and pounded on the glass, calling after him, "Kevin, Kevin, no! Listen to me!" But she knew her cries and blows could barely be heard through the barrier.

Without a backward glance, Kevin disappeared through the prison door.

Tears—of sorrow, of rage, of frustration, but most of all, of love—welled up in her eyes and spilled down her cheeks.

Kevin was the most annoying, most stubborn, most loyal person she knew. He had just turned his back on his only hope. He would rather rot in prison, would rather die there, than allow her to get hurt.

He already looks like death, she thought. She swiped the tears from her eyes and stomped from the room. She could be just as stubborn as he was.

But I'd better hurry, she thought. *Unless I find the evidence I need, and soon, I'm afraid I'll lose him.*

25

Rocky rode up in the elevator of her apartment building, feeling tired and dispirited. She tried to hold on to her anger, tried to let the rage empower her, but the prison visits always left her drained and sad. This time, she felt even worse than usual.

Kevin didn't even try to pretend everything was okay, she thought. *He looked so terrible.*

She stepped from the elevator and trudged down the hall toward her apartment.

If I feel drained after being there for an hour, she told herself, *think how poor Kevin feels.* At least she could leave. Walk through the crowded streets. Breathe fresh air.

She sighed as she unlocked and opened her apartment door. She stepped inside, then stopped abruptly.

Her living room was a maze of interconnected computers and wires, of systems cobbled together from various origins. The jumble of machinery was lit by a single source of flickering light: a computer screen showing design specs displayed in a brilliant spectrum of colors.

"I know I didn't leave that on," she muttered. *Or did I?* she thought. *I've been so distracted lately.*

Absently, she put down her purse and stared at the screen, lost in thought. A light breeze ruffled some papers. Anxious now, she looked around.

The French doors leading to a tiny balcony at the far end of the room were open. "I know I shut those before I left," she said. "It looked like it was going to rain, and I—"

She sensed movement behind her. Adrenaline surged. She lashed out with a back kick, but whoever it was must have dodged. With a sure, fluid motion, she spun, settled into a horse stance, and snapped out a roundhouse kick.

The shadowy figure blocked the blow, then stepped toward the dim light of the computer screen.

Her unwanted visitor was still mostly in silhouette, but she recognized the distinctive cowl with its pointed ears, the flowing cape, the grim mouth and thrusting chin.

"Batman!" She breathed the word. She didn't know if it was a curse or a prayer.

"Nice moves for a bookworm," Batman told her.

She blinked and took a step backward, suddenly becoming flustered. "I used to—I mean—I took self-defense classes, just like a million other women," she stammered.

Then she took a deep breath and fought down her befuddled feeling. After all, she *belonged* here.

"Now it's your turn," she said pointedly. "What are you doing in my apartment?"

Batman gestured at the computer screen, with its light show graphics.

"I've been checking out your new design specs," he said. "If I'm correct, they're several steps beyond what you're doing for WayneTech."

Rocky raised her chin. "You were—, she began. Then started again. "You had no right—"

"Where were you last night?" Batman interrupted in a menacing voice.

He's looming over me deliberately, trying to intimidate me, Rocky told herself. *Well, let him try.*

Angry now, she answered, "I was at WayneTech—"

"No. You left by seven," Batman countered.

Confused, Rocky stammered, "Well, I . . . I went for a walk."

"To the Iceberg Lounge?" Batman snarled the question.

Rocky opened her eyes wide. "Wait a minute—are you trying to say I'm Batwoman?"

She blinked, then looked even more astounded when he didn't deny it. She gasped, "You're not serious!"

Batman held up the piece of tangled metal alloy he had retrieved from the Penguin's office at the Iceberg Lounge.

"Recognize this?" he asked.

Rocky blinked, then nodded. She couldn't take her eyes off the tangle of metal.

"Batwoman used it. It has the same molecular configuration as the alloy you developed for WayneTech."

Rocky took a deep breath. Then she shrugged. "So? I'm hardly the only one working in metallurgy."

"True," Batman said. "But you're the only woman who's the right body type. Plus, you have motive."

Batman picked up the framed photo of Kevin from the computer desk.

Rocky opened her mouth to speak, but no sound came out.

"I know your fiancé was framed for drug smuggling by the Penguin. And I know that someone broke into the Penguin's files recently."

"Yeah? So what?" Rocky said. "Of course I'm trying to get Kevin's sentence commuted. But I'm not doing anything illegal."

She snatched the photo from Batman's hands. Unconsciously protective, she hugged it to her. "Here's a radical notion," she countered. "Instead of investigating me, how about you investigate the bird man? I'll bet there's lots of incriminating evidence on *his* hard drives."

Batman stepped toward the window. "This game you're playing has high stakes—higher than you know," he said. "You could get hurt—or worse."

Rocky stared down at the photo of Kevin. "You sound just like him," she said bitterly.

She looked back up and realized she was alone. The curtain was blowing gently in the night breeze.

"Well, I know what I have to do," she said. She stomped to the French door and slammed it shut with more force than necessary. "And *neither* of you is going to stop me!"

26

The limousine glided majestically through narrow, trash-strewn streets like slumming royalty not amused by the experience.

It slid to a stop in an alley beside a long-deserted brick foundry, much like the other derelict eyesores that crowded this section of the waterfront. Nothing about the factory seemed special. But appearances could be deceiving.

Two men climbed from the limo. The small, plump man was dressed in a tuxedo and carried an umbrella. The taller one shuffled a deck of cards one-handed and glanced around nervously.

"I checked with the warehouse this morning," Rupert Thorne said. "No one reported any trouble."

"Yet." The Penguin gave Thorne a sour look. He glanced down the street. "Ah, there's our cheerful associate now."

A second limo stopped before the plant, and Carleton Duquesne climbed out.

Thorne glanced at Duquesne's face and grimaced. "The guy looks like he could chew nails," he said.

The Penguin shrugged, unconcerned, and waited for Duquesne to join them.

He glanced from one partner to the other. A sly, satisfied smile tilted the corners of his pouty mouth.

"We're all here, gentlemen," the Penguin said. "Shall we meet and greet?"

The Penguin and Thorne turned and walked toward a metal side door. Duquesne rolled his shoulders, as if settling a heavy weight. Then, slowly, he stalked after them.

From her perch atop her jet glider, Batwoman watched the villains enter the abandoned factory.

She steered her glider downward until she was level with the top of the building's huge broken industrial smokestack.

A noise pounded right beside her, making her jump, and she nearly lost her balance on the board. She listened carefully. The sound seemed to be coming from inside the chimney.

Interesting! she thought. *And probably very dangerous! I'd better be careful.*

The three partners walked through patches of afternoon light and shadows, past arcane, long-abandoned equipment.

They too could hear the pounding noise, which was growing louder as they approached the furnace room.

Even though they all knew Bane, either from previous meetings or by reputation, their first sight of him took their breath away.

Bane stood seven feet tall and had muscles on his muscles, and more muscles on those. He was huge, a hyper-massive melange of tubes and brawn, wearing a black sleeveless full bodysuit and full head mask, with openings only for his eyes and mouth.

Tubes ran from his head and body. These, the triumvirate

knew, would carry the drug Venom into his body and allow him to increase his mass and strength as he chose.

Bane was exercising on a makeshift weight machine cobbled together from factory parts and huge slabs of metal. Thick chains ran up over huge pulleys.

Bane was pulling half-ton weights. The pounding sound they had been hearing was the sound of metal slabs hitting makeshift racks.

Everything about the jury-rigged exercise machine was ridiculously overscaled. But then, so was Bane.

Bane lowered the weights when he saw the Penguin and his partners entering the room.

"Penguin," he said in a voice very much at odds with his monstrous appearance. "A pleasure to be doing business with you once again."

Batwoman rappelled on a cable down the interior of the massive chimney.

Any sound I make will be covered by that incessant pounding, she thought. *Whatever it is.*

Then, when she was halfway down, the pounding noise suddenly stopped.

The bottom of the smokestack opened into the large belly of an ancient brick-and-metal furnace. She landed, careful to make no sound.

Voices. And close enough that I can hear them, she thought. *It's about time I got lucky. Now if I can just see who . . .*

For years, rain had poured down the open flue, weakening the mortar, widening cracks, and rusting holes in the furnace door.

At least I have my pick of chinks, she thought. She crouched and peered through one of the holes.

The four men were hard to miss. Especially the hooded, seven-foot-tall monster who called himself Bane.

"I'm sorry," Bane was saying with polished politeness, "but your terms are not acceptable."

Bane wrapped his hands in heavy burlap as he continued speaking. "I want carte blanche—complete control of the operation. I answer to no one."

Duquesne broke in, unable to contain his annoyance. "Now, wait a minute! You can't just waltz in here and start givin' orders—"

While Duquesne ranted, Bane stepped over to a solid steel cylinder hanging from the ceiling like a heavy punching bag. He began to pound it. His fists left big dents in the metal. The remainder of Duquesne's comments faded beneath the metallic clamor.

Only when Duquesne fell silent did Bane continue. "I can't start giving orders, my friend? On the contrary, I can ... and I just did."

He emphasized the point with another drumlike barrage. "Do not worry, Senor Duquesne. If this Batwoman attempts any interference at all—"

Bane planted his feet and hit the cylinder so hard that it tore free from its chain and hurtled across the room, right at the furnace.

Through her crack, Batwoman saw it coming at her like a guided missile. She threw herself flat on the floor as the cylinder plowed into the furnace, smashing through bricks and mortar to lodge halfway inside.

Batwoman lay within the nearly destroyed oven, a bit surprised to find herself still alive. She didn't dare move a muscle now. Discovery would mean the end of all her plans.

Not to mention, if they find me, I'm toast, she thought. *Shape up,* she told herself sternly. *This is no time for misplaced humor. Or hysterics.*

For an instant, she closed her eyes and struggled to still her breathing and calm her racing heart. Then she inched slowly forward on her belly and peered out through the rubble.

Thorne and the Penguin seemed satisfied, she thought. Almost smug. They turned to a subdued-looking Duquesne.

"Now that we've gotten past the niceties, gentlemen, let's discuss the shipment, shall we?" the Penguin said, pulling a folder from his coat pocket.

Within her rubble-strewn hideout, Batwoman silently slid a recorder from her belt. She punched a button; the click made her wince, but the sound didn't seem audible to the four men.

Quietly, she turned its microphone to face the speakers.

The Penguin opened the folder and pulled out a photo.

"The luxury liner SS *Naiad,*" the little man said. "This time we have spared no expense. We're using a luxury cruise liner as our cover. Even better, gentlemen, the ship sails tonight."

No! Batwoman thought from behind her mound of rubble. *It's too soon.*

But as she lay there, she began to figure out what she would need to do to stop them. Her first move, of course, would be to get safely out of the deserted building without being caught.

27

Batman's gloved fist pounded down on the computer stand.

He was seated before his monitor in the Batcave, cape and cowl flung aside, and was feeling as frustrated as he had ever felt.

"What's the matter?" Robin asked, concerned. He stepped behind Bruce's chair and leaned over to have a look at the computer monitor.

Looking annoyed, Batman gestured at the screen.

It was playing a black-and-white videotape, complete with time code and the words *WAYNETECH SECURITY*. The tape showed a wall-cam point-of-view video of Rocky, hard at work in her cubicle. The time code read, 10:34 P.M.

"The night you and I saw Batwoman at the Bric-A-Bracs factory, Rocky Ballentine was working late at WayneTech. The security tapes prove it," Batman said. He sounded disgusted.

"I don't suppose it could have been faked?" Robin asked.

Batman shook his head. "It's totally legit!"

Robin shrugged. "Oh, well. I knew Rocky couldn't be Batwoman. She's too nice."

Alfred stepped into the Batcave, carrying a tea tray.

"First Kathy, then Rocky," Batman grumbled. "Both times I was so sure."

Alfred put down the tray and began to pour a cup of tea for Bruce, then another for Tim. "Well, she can't be in two places at once. Unless she has the power to duplicate herself," Alfred said.

Batman smiled at Alfred's small jest. Then he thought about what Alfred had said, and his eyes widened. With renewed energy, he turned to Robin.

"Robin, get on the computer. I need you to cross-reference all databases on Kathy Duquesne and Roxanne Ballentine. Find anything that connects them. Anything!"

Batman snatched up his cape and cowl and strode toward the Batmobile.

Robin called after him, "Where are you going?"

Batman smiled grimly. "To make a house call," he said.

Batwoman was gliding high above the city on her way to her secret hideout.

It had taken half an hour for the Penguin, Thorne, Duquesne, and their newest partner, Bane, to finalize their plans. Then, after the kingpins had left, Bane also finally prepared to leave.

Batwoman was glad she hadn't tried to rappel back up the chimney with Bane nearby. He was too strong, too big, too dangerous. She didn't want to tangle with him unless she had no choice. That time might come, but she would put it off as long as possible.

Suddenly, she spotted her goal. She swooped downward, and her stomach lurched. She felt almost as if she were in free fall.

She dropped between two derelict buildings and into a dark, cobblestone-covered cul-de-sac.

Ahead of her was a manhole. She flicked a switch on her belt, and as she approached, the manhole cover swiveled open, then lifted.

The arms of the Batglider retracted, and Batwoman sank through the hole and into a long, cylindrical tunnel.

Behind her, the manhole cover slammed shut.

Batwoman sailed into a long-forgotten subway station, dating from the early 1900s. Its design was originally a baroque Dark Deco, and though it had been nearly a century since it had been used, it retained shreds of its previous hard-edged elegance.

Surrounded by its antique opulence, modern technology shone, blinked, beeped, and whirred. Computers had been set up and networked. Lab tables held beakers and retorts, Bunsen burners, even an autoclave. A large wall map of Gotham City covered one wall.

Batwoman leapt lightly from the Batglider as it settled onto the floor. She pulled the recorder from her belt pouch.

"I've got it all here," she said. Her tone was triumphant. "The plans for smuggling the arms—the timetable, the manpower, Bane's agenda—"

"He's on to me," a voice interrupted Batwoman, bringing her down slightly from her victorious high.

Batwoman turned toward the speaker. "What?" she asked. "Rocky—who?"

"Batman," Rocky said. "He knows everything about me—where I work, what I do, all about Kevin. It's uncanny."

Batwoman shrugged. "So what?"

She walked across the room and placed the recorder on a table.

"So what?" Rocky was incredulous. "He's going to ruin

everything! I told you we should've created a new identity for our heroine persona, not just spun it off Batman's."

"She's right." Kathy Duquesne lounged against a table. "Look at how fast he caught on to *me*. We didn't count on this."

Again Batwoman shrugged. "So he thinks you're the Batwoman, Rocky. Big deal."

Batwoman turned to Kathy. "Look, two days ago he thought it was Kathy! Tomorrow we'll have him thinking it's someone else."

Batwoman pulled off her mask so that she could look her friends in the eye. "Trust me! If Batman really had any idea what was going on, I would know."

Kathy was partially mollified, but couldn't resist a dig. "Easy for you to be cool, Alcana."

Rocky folded her arms and said emphatically, "Yeah, Sonia. *You* haven't been in the hot seat yet."

Sonia Alcana threw up her hands in a what-can-I-tell-you? gesture. "I know, guys, but we're so close to our goal! We stop them tonight and we've broken them."

"Tonight?" Kathy croaked.

Rocky folded her arms. "They're moving that fast?"

"Not too fast for us, Rocky." Sonia's smile was a devilish smirk. "*Never* too fast for us."

28

Dusk had just fallen over the city when Batman climbed silently through the window of Kathy Duquesne's bedroom. He was hoping to find a clue, any clue, that would link her to Rocky Ballentine.

They're working together, he thought. *They have to be!*

Kathy's bedroom was tastefully, if lavishly, furnished with richly colored fabrics, plush carpet, and a dressing table strewn with makeup and perfume bottles. It was the room of a woman who, like the song said, enjoyed being a girl.

Across from a bed piled high with silky pillows hung a charming double portrait. A woman with her arm protectively around a young girl's shoulder. The two were looking lovingly into each other's laughing eyes, as if they were sharing a private joke.

No question about their identities, Batman thought. Kathy—who looked around ten—and her late mother, who looked much the way her beautiful daughter did now.

Checking closely, Batman noted the artist's signature. *Emaline Duquesne.* Kathy's mother had painted the picture and had caught the love she and her daughter shared. The mother had been a skilled artist, indeed.

And this beloved woman had been blown away before Kathy's eyes.

An event like that could warp a person, Batman thought, *could make them lose perspective.* He personally had reason to know.

Batman hadn't known whom to blame for his own parents' deaths. But Kathy did.

Duquesne had kept the nature of his employment from Kathy's mother. In Kathy's opinion, he had tricked her mother into marrying him. And her mother had been shot because she was standing at his side.

How much does Kathy hate her father? Batman wondered. *How far will she go to punish him?*

Batman turned from the portrait to study the rest of the room.

He searched through Kathy's bureau drawers, then checked her desk, looking for anything that might help him prove the connection he was sure was there.

Suddenly, Kathy's bedroom door creaked open. A wedge of light from the hall beyond flooded the room. Batman looked up from the desk drawer he was searching.

Wilbur stuck his head into the room. "Hey, somebody in here?" he asked gruffly.

Batman rose to his full height, folded his arms, and glared. Wilbur froze, staring into Batman's slitted eyes.

One of Wilbur's own baby blues was still bruised, and his nose was skewed to the left from his last encounter with the Dark Knight. Wilbur's mouth formed a silent "Oh!" Then, without a word, he backed out of the room and quietly closed the door behind him.

Batman heard more footsteps in the hall outside. "Hey, Wilbur," a voice said. "Anything wrong?"

"Not a thing, Chic," Wilbur said with absolute conviction. "Not a thing!"

Batman smiled grimly. It seemed Wilbur had finally learned not to go looking for trouble. Just as well, Batman thought. He had better things to do with his time than teach refresher courses in Let Well Enough Alone 101.

Not that the time spent here so far had netted him much, he thought, discouraged. Then he noticed the decorative screen in the corner of Kathy's room.

Batman checked behind it and found another door. He opened it.

The doorway led to a small artist's studio.

One wall held a bookcase piled with books and drawing pads of different shapes and sizes.

In a corner stood an easel, covered in a dusty cloth. Batman pulled off the material and found a painting of the gnarled tree on the cliff where he and Kathy had stopped to talk.

Same style as the portrait, Batman thought. Kathy had said the cliff had been her mother's favorite place to paint.

Batman pulled one of the black leather-bound books from the shelf. The top edge was dust-covered. Batman blew off the dust, then flipped through the pages. *A sketchbook,* he thought. *That of a young child, but one with talent.*

He skimmed through another sketchbook and saw that halfway through, Kathy had begun to sign her name.

He looked quickly through the next book, saw that young Kathy had begun to develop her own stylized signature.

Each book showed increasingly sophisticated drawings. Toward the end of the collection, some even held dates.

The drawings in the final sketchbook in the series were made the year Kathy's mother died.

After that, there were no more leather-bound books filled with childish drawings. *Kathy must have given up art after the trauma of her mother's death,* Batman thought. *At least for a while.*

Next on the shelf were several large newsprint sketch pads.

The first held early model drawings done in charcoal. Probably from late high school or early college. *Art 101 stuff,* he thought. But the sketches showed definite promise.

He opened another of the large newsprint pads and found a self-portrait—or maybe a drawing of her mother copied from a photograph.

He picked up a third sketch pad. This one had the name of a college supply shop printed in a corner.

A buzzing sound jerked Batman from his search. He tapped a point on the side of his head near his ear. "Yes," he snapped.

Robin's voice came through the earpiece. "I got some bad news for you," he said. "Or maybe good, depending."

"Spit it out!" Batman growled. He continued flipping through pages in the newsprint pads as Robin's voice continued. "There's no connection between Kathy and Rocky. Different cities. Different circles. Different planets."

Batman stopped and stared at a sketch as Robin's voice continued. "There's just no way they would've known each other."

"Yes there is!" Batman's voice held a *Eureka!* quality.

Page after page of the sketchbook in his hands held drawings of a younger Sonia Alcana. The work was sophisticated, the likeness unmistakable. In a gruff voice, he continued, "All they needed was someone to introduce them."

29

The computer monitor screens that lined Batwoman's underground headquarters held different diagrammatic angles of the schematics to the SS *Naiad.*

Sonia Alcana, now dressed for work, sat before a computer keyboard.

"Remember, once they load the ships, Bane will station himself in the pilot cabin, here," she said. She hit several keys on the computer keyboard. Immediately, red lights, representing Bane, appeared on the different schematics.

"Guards will be placed at checkpoints around the deck," Sonia continued, and typed in several other commands. Blue dots appeared, marking the location of the guards.

Sonia glanced up at Kathy, who was now wearing the Batwoman leotard and cape. Kathy was leaning over Sonia's shoulder, memorizing the locations on the screen.

"You get past this guard," Sonia said, and one of the blue lights began to blink. "Then it's a straight shot to the Atrium, where the bulk of the weapons are kept."

Kathy pulled on a red leather glove and grinned wickedly. "Not to mention the spectacular gift boutiques."

Rocky held out a rectangular box about the size of a laptop. "This is the bomb," she said. "The detonator has a fail-safe countdown. I wouldn't shop too long."

"Got ya!" Kathy said. She took the bomb in her gloved hands and slipped it into a carry bag hidden beneath her cape.

Then she looked at the others with an air of finality. "I guess this is it," Kathy told them.

Sonia sighed. "I just wish it was me this time."

Kathy pulled on the cowl, with its gauzy face covering. "You have to go to work," she said. "Besides, it's my turn to play dress-up."

She fiddled with the control on her belt, and the Batglider flew toward her. It hovered in the air near knee level.

Kathy climbed onto the glider, knelt, and, with a cheery wave, soared upward. The manhole cover slid open, and Kathy Duquesne, aka Batwoman, flew out into the night.

Kathy rode her glider above the city. She was heading toward the SS *Naiad* and its meeting with destiny.

She heard the blast of the ship's horn before she reached the harbor. The *Naiad,* already out of its berth, was sailing toward the deep channel that led beneath the Gotham Bay Bridge and out into the ocean.

Guess I'm running a minute or so behind, Kathy thought. She gunned the Batglider, racing to catch up with her quarry.

From her aerial vantage point, Kathy could clearly see the various decks: the sun and sports decks, with jogging tracks, volleyball and shuffleboard courts, outdoor swimming pools, and, nearby, the domed skylight, now illuminated from inside by the lights from the Atrium. Below were the verandah, lido, promenade, and other decks. Kathy hadn't expected the cruise ship to be so brightly lit, as if it were thronged with eager passengers.

Their research had shown that the liner was a recent acquisition of the Penguin's. It would go down with all their illegal armaments, and that would make victory all the sweeter.

She circled the *Naiad* on her glider, just checking it out. If there was some mistake—if the Penguin had brought innocent civilians aboard—they would have to abort their mission.

But all Kathy saw were a few thugs and goons in uniforms, most of whom she recognized as members of the Penguin's Iceberg Lounge pack. These were stationed at the rails, right where Sonia had said they'd be. It was no surprise that those guards carried some of the Penguin's contingent of outlandish super-weapons.

Kathy guided her jet board lower until she was cruising silently above the pilot's cabin. Through the window, she spotted two thuggish mercenary types in pilot's uniforms at the wheel. Bane, standing behind them, gazed out into the darkness.

Sonia had not exaggerated, Kathy thought. Bane was huge. Monumental. Almost breathtaking. The pilots looked like children standing beside him.

Bane's head moved, chin raised just a trifle, and Kathy's heart clutched. For an instant, she was sure she had been spotted.

She slowed her glider, peeled off to one side, and watched the patrolling guards. No one came to alert or began to search the night sky with weapons at ready.

Guess everything's cool, she thought with relief. *We're much too close to blow it now!*

Bane was a big brute, but size wasn't necessarily an advantage, she told herself bracingly. It made him easy to spot and hard to hide. For now, she knew, Bane was in the pilot's cabin.

She'd pray he stayed there. But she'd keep her eyes open, just in case.

Kathy silently sky-surfed toward the lido deck, where a guard was pacing, protecting a doorway. When his back was toward Kathy, she leapt from the Batglider and kicked him to the ground. The goon was unconscious before he realized he was under attack.

Kathy stepped over his body and opened the door, which led into a corridor.

Following the plan Sonia had devised, Kathy slipped down the hallway and dashed toward the Atrium.

She entered at level three and leaned over the high brass railing to check out the place.

The Atrium was cylindrical and multistoried, with seven decks opening onto the vaulting space, and shops and restaurants on each level. Leaning over the rail and looking up, she could see the domed skylight. Down below, she noticed crates of varying shapes, sizes, and materials, neatly stacked in the shopping plaza.

A cylindrical transparent glass elevator was resting on the bottom floor.

No one seemed to be guarding any of the levels. *Good,* she thought. *That will make my job easier.*

She removed a hook-ended cable from her belt pouch, angled it over the railing, and rappelled down toward the main landing.

When she reached the bottom, she noticed that the shops there were also filled with crates. *All in all, quite the little shipment,* Kathy thought.

She moved among the crates like a wraith, making sure no

one was lurking there. She noticed that several large missile launchers had simply been propped up against the stacks.

"What, you can build 'em but you couldn't find a box big enough to hold 'em?" she muttered. She looked around and spotted a large metal crate that looked about the right size. "What about this one?"

Yeah, what about *that one?* she thought. *Right size, right shape, right material to act as anchor for the bomb.*

Kathy reached into her carry pack and pulled out the explosive device. She crouched, ready to attach the bomb to the largest crate.

She heard a metallic clang and whirled, heart beating like a trip-hammer, but it was only the Atrium clock, balanced on a decorative pole, chiming as it hit the hour.

She closed her eyes and sighed with relief.

Again she crouched, pushing the buttons that would set the timer. After that she would attach the bomb magnetically to the steel crate and initiate the countdown.

Two minutes, she thought. *That's how long I'll have to get off the ship.*

Suddenly, the walls of the metal crate exploded outward.

Kathy fell back with a startled cry of alarm.

A dark, hulking behemoth was rising from the box in which he had been crouching.

Bane! Kathy thought. *That freak must have spotted me, after all. He was hidden inside the crate, waiting for me. It was a trap!*

"Senorita," Bane said, his tone urbane, almost amused.

Stung by his attitude, Kathy kicked out at Bane, but only hurt her foot. Gasping in pain and surprise, she realized it was like kicking a brick wall.

A moment later, she was flying backward, the victim of a

120

brisk backhand blow. She crashed so hard into a pile of smaller crates that she splintered the wood.

Bane strode toward her. He was reaching for her. Kathy tried to prop herself up, but the blow had been too disabling.

Blackness edged her sight, then grew all-encompassing.

Bane lifted the Batwoman up by her cape and pulled off her mask.

Then he reached for his cell phone.

30

Atop the Roost, in the Penguin's well-appointed den, Rupert Thorne and the Penguin sat at a card table playing gin rummy. Nearby, Carleton Duquesne slouched in an easy chair, nervously drumming a pencil against a side table.

The Penguin scowled at him.

"Would you stop that infernal tapping?" he grumbled. "What are you so nervous about? In a few minutes, the ship will be in international waters, and we'll all be much richer than we are already."

He slapped a card down on the table and chortled, "Gin!"

The ringer on the Penguin's old-fashioned phone jangled shrilly. For a moment, everyone froze. Then the Penguin picked up the receiver.

"Yes, he's here," the others heard the Penguin say. The little man glanced pointedly at Duquesne. "We're all here."

Thorne and Duquesne looked at each other, silently asking, *What now?*

The Penguin listened. He opened his mouth in an astonished little *O,* then asked, "She did?" Then, "No!" He paused, then he asked, "You want us now?"

The Penguin hung up the phone, amazement still clear on his face. He looked at Duquesne again.

Duquesne was standing now, feeling apprehensive. He didn't know what was up, but he figured it couldn't be anything good. For him, at least.

"Is the ship—" Duquesne began worriedly.

The Penguin flapped both hands, signaling Duquesne to simmer down. "The ship's fine," he said. "But Bane isn't letting it leave the harbor yet. He wants us to come aboard." The Penguin waited, letting the suspense build. Finally, he announced, "It appears, gentlemen, that Bane has captured Batwoman."

Sonia Alcana was waiting on the roof of Gotham City Police Headquarters, beside the unlit Bat-Signal spotlight. She had chosen that vantage point because it allowed a good view of the river that flowed beneath the Gotham Bay Bridge, into the bay, and out into the open ocean.

Through her binoculars, Sonia had been studying the brightly lit SS *Naiad*. And waiting. To receive some word from Kathy that things had gone according to plan. And to witness the explosion that would sink the *Naiad* and destroy the fortune of Rupert Thorne.

But no word had come from Kathy. To make matters even more worrisome, the *Naiad* had halted midway to the bridge, still brightly lit and festive looking, but unmoving.

"This isn't good," she whispered. "Something must've gone wrong."

Catching silent movement behind her, Sonia turned.

"Batman," she said.

For a moment, he simply stood there, looking down at her. Behind his mask, Batman's eyes were piercing and accusatory. "You knew Kathy Duquesne," he said.

"What?" Sonia asked, feigning confusion. The moment she saw him, she had known they were busted; but she decided to play for time, to not surrender without at least a token fight.

"You two took an art class together. She sketched your face. Enough times to make me believe you were more than mere acquaintances," Batman said.

He pulled the sketchbook from a pouch inside his cape and dropped it flat on the ground at Sonia's feet. "It was years ago, but it's clearly you. Kathy had a good eye. You also knew Rocky Ballentine," he continued.

"Who?" Sonia asked, wide-eyed, not giving Batman an inch.

"Let me jog your memory," Batman said. "State university. Freshman year. Same dorm. Same floor. Same room."

Sonia smiled bitterly. "Rocky said you were uncanny."

"Each of you brought something to the party," Batman concluded. "Kathy had the money, Rocky had the genius, and you—you had the scheme, and the will to make it happen."

Sonia looked into the distance, remembering. "When that fire destroyed my folks' business, they never recovered. They'd worked their whole lives to have it, and then it was all gone, just like that.

"But the human toll was worse. My father had a stroke and became half-paralyzed. My mother had inhaled a lot of smoke. Her health was never good after that. Both were too old, too ill to rebuild.

"It tore our family apart."

Sonia paused. "Everyone knew Rupert Thorne had ordered the arson because my parents refused to pay protection money. But there was no way to prove it. Now Thorne is going to know how it feels to see his life go up in smoke."

"Three women, three motives. Three Batwomen," Batman said grimly. "It was just a matter of disguising your voices and taking turns. And you know what? It almost worked."

As Batman spoke, he saw Sonia's hand stray slowly toward the shoulder holster hidden beneath her jacket.

He heard the soft click as she released the flap. *Is she really going to try to pull that gun on me?* he wondered. *Is she really that desperate for revenge?*

For a moment, Sonia stood on the roof of Police HQ, her hand resting on her pistol.

Kathy's still aboard the Naiad. *I can't let Batman stop her from placing the bomb,* she thought. *But I can't pull a gun on Batman either. He saved my life.* For a moment, she stood there, pulled in two directions. Both choices were right . . . and both were wrong.

Her cell phone rang, snapping her from her reverie.

Instead of the pistol, she pulled her cell phone from her inside jacket pocket.

"I'm here," Sonia said.

"Something is definitely wrong." Over the receiver, Sonia could hear Rocky's voice quaver. Sonia could picture Rocky pacing across their headquarters as the computer screens displayed information and statistics telling her what Sonia could see with her own eyes.

"There's no report from the Coast Guard of any ship in distress," Rocky said. "I radioed Kathy, but she's not responding. She's in trouble, Sonia. I can feel it! What are we going to do?"

Rocky sounds as worried as I am, Sonia thought. She glanced at Batman, wondering if she dared take him into her confidence.

She looked again at the *Naiad,* still riding in the bay, and decided that she had no choice. Kathy's safety was more important than their revenge.

"Rocky," Sonia said into the phone. "I think we'd better rethink our plan. . . ."

31

A jaunty speedboat, sculpted and painted to look like a penguin slicing through the water on its belly, jounced and bounced over the choppy water toward the SS *Naiad* lying at anchor in the middle of Gotham Bay.

The Penguin steered the small racer with his right hand while he held on to his top hat with his left. Rupert Thorne and Carleton Duquesne were ensconced behind him in the passenger seats.

The speedboat neared the rear of the resting *Naiad,* and Duquesne spotted the small docking bay set into the cruise ship's stern. An armed guard was waiting there.

"Throw him the line, would you, Mr. Duquesne?" the Penguin requested.

Duquesne picked up a coil of rope and tossed it to the guard. The goon secured the speedboat, and the three kingpins clambered aboard the *Naiad.*

"Excellent," the Penguin said, brushing together his gloved hands. "Now, where can we find Bane?"

* * *

Neither the criminal triumvirate nor the guards noticed when the submersible Batboat slowly emerged from the surface of the bay and silently cruised toward the *Naiad.*

Robin sat in the captain's chair, piloting the submersible. Batman stood, binoculars focused through the Batboat's bubble-top windscreen, studying the cruise ship.

"Interesting," Batman said. "The Penguin, Thorne, and Duquesne have all gone aboard. That's not part of the plan. Something's definitely up!"

Robin sighed. "And that probably isn't good news for Kathy Duquesne."

The Penguin, Thorne, and Duquesne stared down through the cylindrical glass wall of the elevator as it descended toward the bottom floor of the Atrium.

Bane looked up, waiting for them. Batwoman's Utility Belt was slung over one of his massive shoulders.

Behind Bane, Batwoman stood, her face hooded, her stance defiant. Her hands were cuffed behind her back, and one of Bane's guards held her by the arms, to make extra-certain that she couldn't escape.

"She doesn't look so tough now, does she, Thorne?" the Penguin asked, rubbing his gloved hands together as he gleefully anticipated the upcoming interview. Thorne seemed equally eager to reach the bottom floor.

By contrast, something about the hooded figure gave Carleton Duquesne a sharp pain in the pit of his stomach. *Bane caught Batwoman!* he thought. *The shipment's safe. I'm going to recoup my fortune. I should be over the moon about this. So what's wrong with me?*

Maybe it's just that so much is riding on this deal, he thought. He wasn't normally given to baseless apprehension.

But something told him he wasn't going to like how the up-coming interview played out—and it was a gut feeling he just couldn't shake.

The Penguin stepped from the elevator with Thorne and Duquesne following close on his heels.

To judge by the way Thorne's reshuffling his cards, maybe he's as nervous as I am, Duquesne realized. It was a reassuring thought.

The Penguin strode toward Bane. "Bravo, senor," he said. "Exemplary work."

Bane nodded graciously. "I wanted you here when I realized who she was," he said. "I felt a certain caution was in order."

Thorne wrinkled his brow. "So who is she?" he asked.

Bane grabbed the mask and yanked it off.

The Penguin scowled.

Thorne fumbled his shuffle, and the cards spilled onto the floor.

Duquesne gasped. "Kathy?"

32

When her father saw Kathy's wan face above the Batwoman costume, his own face had paled. Horror was evident in his trembling voice. "Kathy!" he gasped again.

The Penguin turned on Duquesne in a fury. "What's going on?" he snarled.

"No wonder Batwoman always knew our plans!" Thorne growled.

"What? You think I told her?" Duquesne sounded indignant. But his eyes looked glassy, as if he was in shock. "I know nothin' about any of this!"

Bane held up a flat rectangular box. "This is what she planned to detonate. Don't let the size fool you, senors; it's a carbonite bomb. It can take out this entire chamber and more."

Bane placed the bomb on a crate.

Duquesne leaned toward his daughter. Suddenly, his eyes were sparking with anger. "Are you crazy?" he shouted. "How could you do this to me?"

Kathy sneered. "It was easy, Daddy. You made it easy because of the kind of man you are. The kind whose wife is killed just because she stands next to him. The kind who makes a fortress out of his own house and a prisoner out of his own child. The kind who destroys lives for profit. And whose real loyalty is to scum like them!"

Kathy's glance flicked over the Penguin and Thorne dismissively.

Duquesne's hand tightened into a fist. "Shut up!" he screamed at his daughter.

He turned to the Penguin. "This doesn't make sense!"

The Penguin met Duquesne's eyes. "On that we agree," he said. "Because I distinctly remember your daughter being at my lounge the same night that Batwoman assaulted me. Obviously, she *can't* be Batwoman—at least, not *all* the time."

He turned to Kathy, bringing the tip of his umbrella up until it almost touched the tip of her nose. "Who else is involved?" he asked.

There was a hissing sound. Then a waft of vapor rose from the tip of the umbrella.

"Acid, my dear," the Penguin said. "A vapor to destroy your lungs . . . or a stream to destroy your countenance. But avoidable . . . if you answer the question."

Kathy pulled back, trying to turn her head away.

"No!" Duquesne shouted. He lunged forward, grabbed the umbrella, and forced it away from his daughter's face.

Then Bane's huge arm was around Duquesne's neck and chest, pulling the gangster backward.

"You're out, Duquesne," Thorne said with a sneer.

"I never shoulda gotten mixed up with garbage like you!" Duquesne choked out.

"The pot calling the kettle black?" Kathy Duquesne taunted. *What's wrong with me?* she thought, ashamed and confused. *I can't stop taunting Daddy, even when he's trying to save me.*

The Penguin sneered. "Well, that will give you something to

130

talk about in family therapy, won't it? Assuming either of you lives long enough to get there."

Duquesne could say no more as the breath was literally being squeezed from him. He grabbed at Bane's hand, trying to force it away from his throat. But strong and powerful though Duquesne was, he was no match for the massive super-soldier.

Duquesne couldn't talk. Couldn't breathe.

"No!" Kathy screamed. "Don't! He didn't know. Don't hurt him."

This time, the Penguin thrust the tip of the umbrella against Duquesne's cheek. "Then tell me who else is involved," he said. "While Daddy here still has a face."

Kathy hesitated. For herself, it no longer mattered. Whatever happened, she was as good as dead. But maybe she could save the others.

But which *others?* she asked herself, in near despair. *Who should I save? If I tell him Rocky and Sonia are involved in this, the Penguin will kill them too. And if I don't, he'll kill my father.*

She swept her eyes around the soaring Atrium, searching desperately for a way out of her impossible dilemma. And caught her breath.

High above, on an upper-floor railing, Batman was crouched like a vulture.

Before Kathy's startled response could give him away, the Dark Knight jumped off the railing and swung toward the main floor. With his cape flaring like wings behind him, he slammed, feetfirst, into Bane's back.

Unprepared for the impact, Bane lurched forward, releasing Duquesne as he threw out his arms in an effort to regain his balance. Then, with a grunt of surprise, Bane pitched to his knees.

Batman rolled away from Bane and rose smoothly to his feet.

Duquesne crawled several feet from his captor, then collapsed, gasping for air.

Thorne reached beneath his suit jacket and pulled out his pistol, but a Batarang hit his hand and sent the weapon flying.

Batman raised another Batarang, but before he could throw it, Bane had leapt to his feet and spin-kicked out at him.

Batman flew backward. He slammed with a grunt of pain into the elevator, and the cylinder cracked beneath the impact.

The Penguin, now holding his umbrella pointed at the captive Kathy, watched the combat closely. Even he winced at the force of Batman's collision with the glass.

Batman slid to the ground. He swiped his gloved hand across his face, rubbing a trickle of blood from the corner of his mouth.

Bane stalked toward the Dark Knight. His fists, massive as sledgehammers, raised to pound Batman into dust.

"Bon voyage, Señor Batman," Bane said.

33

Bane brought his fists down to crush Batman, but in a practiced move, the Dark Knight reached into his belt pouch and hurled a handful of pellets into the super-soldier's face. As the pellets exploded into smoke, Batman rolled aside, and Bane's fists shattered the elevator instead.

Batman slammed Bane with a double-legged kick to the ribs.

Smoke from the pellets spread, enveloping the Penguin, Thorne, and Kathy's startled guard.

Taking advantage of her guard's momentary distraction, Kathy, hands still cuffed behind her back, jerked down and rearward, breaking her captor's hold on her. She swept into a spin kick, hitting the guard in the back and knocking him forward into the horrified Penguin. They slammed together with muffled grunts of surprise.

Kathy jumped into the air, bringing her knees up and together, and swung her cuffed hands beneath her body and up to her front.

The Penguin regained his balance, pointed his umbrella tip, and fired off a spray of acid. Kathy dove aside into the smoke from Batman's pellets, and the spray struck the Atrium clock, which sizzled and smoked, then melted.

She rolled sideways, taking advantage of the smoke screen, and kicked out at the Penguin's knees. She connected, and he fell backward with a squawk, disappearing into the smoke.

"Good try." Kathy heard the menace in Thorne's voice.

On her feet now, she turned. Through the billowing smoke, she saw that Thorne was standing in front of her, pointing a bazooka laser at the middle of her chest.

Suddenly, a dark shape was flying at her through the haze. Batman, grasping his grappling cable with one hand, snatched up Kathy with the other.

Thorne fired after them. Laser blasts from the bazooka scored deep fissures in the walls as Thorne shot again and again.

He's getting too close, Batman thought. *We've got to get out of his line of sight. Now!*

As a laser blast burned a hole in his cape, Batman let go of the grappling line, and he and Kathy tumbled forward, over the railing of the third-floor terrace and onto the carpet beyond.

Thorne flicked a switch to widen the range of the blast, pointed the nozzle toward the terrace at the spot where Batman and Kathy had landed, and pulled the trigger.

Batman shoved Kathy down the corridor as the terrace behind them disappeared in an explosion of light and noise.

Kathy and Batman dashed down the hallway as laser blasts from below ricocheted around them.

In the Atrium, Thorne stopped firing.

Bane was shouting into his communicator. "Bane to bridge.

Weigh anchor and head out to sea! We must be in international waters as quickly as possible."

"Aye, sir," the pilot answered. "We're on our way."

As Duquesne struggled to his feet, he could feel the vibrations of the engines as the ship began to move through the bay toward the open sea.

34

The submersible Batboat was lying just under the water's surface. Robin was still at the wheel. His part in the operation was to make sure the Penguin and his cohorts didn't get away.

Suddenly, the *Naiad*'s huge propellers began to spin, creating a swirling vortex and a blinding foam of bubbles. For an instant, the Batboat was sucked toward the powerful spinning blades.

Then Robin threw the engine of the submersible into reverse.

For long seconds, Robin feared the engine of the smaller craft would be too weak, that the Batboat would be sucked into the whirling vortex and smashed against the huge propellers.

He pulled on the wheel with all his strength, trying to turn the Batboat as he fought the current. Finally, the submersible slid out of harm's way.

Robin brought the Batboat to the surface, and as it emerged from the water, he realized that the *Naiad* was heading for the Gotham Gate Bridge. The graceful suspension bridge rested on two footings sunk deep into the floor of the river and supported a high midsection arch.

Robin knew a ship the size of the *Naiad* could pass beneath the center span easily. Beyond the span lay the open ocean.

In the air above the *Naiad,* Rocky Ballentine and Sonia Alcana, both in Batwoman leotards and cloaks, hovered on identical Batgliders. For now, they had removed their masks.

"What's the point of concealment?" Sonia had asked her friend. Plain and simple, they were busted.

Rocky had sighed and answered that in some ways it was a relief.

Now, with the wind tossing her golden curls, Rocky shouted, "The ship's heading to sea. What do you think?"

"Batman said he'd give us a signal," Sonia answered, "but that doesn't mean we can't take a closer look."

Sonia pushed several windswept auburn strands from her eyes. "Busted or not, this, at least, is another reason to wear a mask," she said.

They exchanged amused grins, then pulled down their hoods to obscure their features *and* secure their hair.

Then, crouching on their gliders, they swooped down toward the ship.

The smoke in the Atrium had almost dissipated when Duquesne stumbled to his feet, rubbing his still-sore neck. He looked angrily at the others.

"You had no right." He was still breathless, and his voice was hoarse.

"And you have no say, Duquesne!" Thorne growled. "Not any longer!"

The Penguin dusted off his hands and restored his monocle

to his eye socket. "Indeed, we have a lot more to worry about than your parental neglect," he said.

With his monocle adjusted, he looked around.

"Where's the bomb?" the Penguin asked. "Wasn't it right there?" He pointed to the crate upon which Bane had placed the bomb earlier. It was empty.

Bane stepped forward and saw that the bomb was, indeed, gone. Beneath his mask, the line of his mouth grew even grimmer.

Bane shot out a hand and, once again, grabbed Duquesne. He said one word through gritted teeth. "Bait."

The metal door to the engine room burst open, and Batman rushed inside. Kathy followed.

The chamber was huge and cavernous, reaching from the bottom hull to the top deck, where a huge funnel channeled the exhaust from the boiler room engines out the top of the ship.

Above their heads were catwalks and metal stairways attached to the exterior smokestack. The engines were throbbing, an earsplitting cacophony of metal pounding against metal.

Batman grabbed Kathy by her joined wrists and used a Batknife to open the cuffs. As the restraint fell from her right wrist, Kathy shouted over the clamor of the generators, "I could have gotten out of them."

"No doubt," Batman shouted back. "Since you got yourself into them."

The remark stung. *So he thinks I'm incompetent,* Kathy thought, an angry thrust to her jaw. *Well, I'll show him.*

As the cuff fell from Kathy's left wrist, Batman looked toward the ceiling. He lifted a grappling hook.

"Your friends are waiting to rescue you," he said. "Let's not disappoint them."

He aimed upward and fired.

As he looked up and away from her, Kathy slid the bomb from inside her cape. She pressed it against the steel generator wall, where it magnetically adhered.

She had already set the counter. All she had to do now was push the button that began the countdown.

"No," Kathy shouted as she activated the counter. "Let's not!"

Her smug tone caught Batman's attention. He glanced back at her and saw the bomb clinging to the engine wall.

The timer, which had been at 2:00, began to count down: 1:59 . . . 1:58 . . . 1:57 . . .

35

Glaring at Kathy, Batman reached out to detach the bomb from the wall of the generator.

Kathy grabbed his arm, forcing his hand back while she shouted at him. "Don't! Break magnetic contact and it will go off. And there's no way to stop the countdown without the code . . . which escapes me at present."

At that moment, she looked so smug, Batman thought. So arrogant. In some odd way, so like her father.

Batman grabbed her arm roughly and growled, "You can't—"

"I'm sorry," Kathy said. "But one way or another, it has to end."

Batman looked into her eyes and knew she would rather die than relent. Like her father, once she was set on a course, she was unyielding and impervious to reason.

Not that he had much time to reason with her anyway.

The clock was at 1:50 now and counting down. 1:49.

The bomb was going to go off, he realized, and there was nothing he could do to stop it.

With a grunt of angry resignation, Batman grabbed Kathy

roughly around the waist. The cable retracted, pulling him and Kathy up together.

The Penguin and Thorne, who was carrying a bazooka laser, clambered down a stairway and into the *Naiad*'s small docking bay. The penguin-shaped speedboat was tied there as they had left it.

They clambered into it hastily.

"Even if Batwoman doesn't have the bomb, an expeditious retreat is probably our most prudent move," the Penguin said.

Thorne fired his weapon, cutting through the mooring line as the Penguin revved the speedboat engine.

"Well, whattaya know," they heard a female voice say. "Our two favorite felons."

The Penguin and Thorne looked up. Just outside the docking bay, they saw two Batwomen hovering on identical Batgliders.

"Egads!" the Penguin squawked. "They're multiplying."

Before the Penguin could raise his umbrella, Rocky pitched a Batangle that pierced his sleeve, pinning it against the dashboard of the boat.

The Penguin squeaked shrilly.

Thorne hefted his bazooka to fire, but Sonia hurled several Batangles. They sliced into his hand, and Thorne dropped the weapon with a bellow of pain and anger.

Sonia glided a bit closer. "You can't imagine how good that felt, Thorne," Sonia said. "Now, where is Kathy Duquesne?"

Batman and Kathy were pulled up to a high catwalk. They raced out a door and emerged onto the top sporting deck, below the funnel, right next to the outdoor swimming pool.

Kathy looked around for her co-Batwomen, but no one was in sight. She could neither call them nor summon her glider, since Bane had taken her Utility Belt with all its handy gadgets.

"The bomb's still ticking," she said to Batman. "We have a little over a minute before it blows. Which way now?"

Suddenly, there was a movement overhead. They looked up, hoping that the cavalry had arrived.

No such luck.

Carleton Duquesne, wrapped round with a heavy linked chain, was swinging in an arc, back and forth like a pendulum above their heads. The chain from which the kingpin dangled led up fifty feet to one of the thick, aerodynamic fins that decorated the cruise ship's single funnel.

The monstrous Bane clutched the other end of the chain, swinging the terrified Duquesne back and forth in ever-higher arcs. The rest of the long length of the chain was wrapped diagonally across Bane's body.

Ignoring Kathy, Bane spoke to Batman. "I knew sooner or later we would face each other, Batman. I have prayed for it."

Bane swung Duquesne back and forth, higher and higher. Then, as if Duquesne were a worm on the end of a fisherman's line, Bane cast him into the swimming pool.

Kathy rushed to the railing. For an instant, she watched, horrified, as her father splashed into the pool. Then, weighted by the heavy links of steel, he sank quickly to the bottom.

"Daddy!" Kathy screamed. "No!"

Without a thought for her own safety, she recklessly dove into the water after him.

* * *

142

Batman looked up at Bane and saw that he still held one end of the chain that bound Duquesne. By Bane's stance, Batman could tell that the super-soldier had no intention of pulling the kingpin from the water. Now that Duquesne had fulfilled his purpose, Bane would let him die without another thought.

Batman fired a cable-trailing grapnel. It slammed into the funnel above Bane's head, and sharp hooked teeth bit into the sheet metal. Then, when the grapnel was securely fastened, Batman punched the retractor button and was dragged upward instantly. As he neared the funnel, he let go of the cable and dropped onto the fin, facing his massive opponent.

"I'm warning you, Bane," Batman said. "In less than a minute, this ship is going down."

"Then you've made my choice easy," Bane said. "If there is nothing I can do about the ship, then I choose to place my full attention on destroying you."

36

Taking a deep breath, Kathy swam downward. Her father had fallen into the deepest part of the pool. She could see him resting on the bottom, weighted down by the heavy links of steel.

He was moving, struggling to free himself, so she knew he was still alive. But how long could he last? She would have to act quickly if she was going to save him.

Kathy reached her father. She grabbed hold of the chain binding her father's arms to his sides and pulled as hard as she could. If she could just loosen them, she thought, then her father could wiggle free and swim to the surface.

But the chain was wound too tightly and locked in place by a huge, solid padlock. To her frustrated horror, Kathy couldn't budge either.

This is my fault, she thought bitterly. *I blamed my father for causing the death of my mother. I tried to pay him back for that and every wrong he's ever done in his life. And now, because of what I've done, he's going to die.*

I can't let that happen! she thought desperately. *If I can't free him, then, somehow, I've got to get him to the surface.*

She put her arms around him and strained to swim upward. The blessed air was only eight feet, maybe nine feet, above their heads, but it might as well have been a mile. The heavy chain was a dead weight. She couldn't move him.

And they both were running out of air.

Kathy could see the panic, the dawning horror on her father's face. Knew it must mirror the look on her own. Knew that, because of what she had done, her own father was going to drown.

My fault, my fault. The blood pounding in her ears beat out the refrain.

I'm my father's daughter more than I ever was my gentle, loving mother's. What I hate in him is what I hate in myself. We're ruthless and thoughtless. We see what we want and go after it and never think about the consequences . . . ever . . . until it's too late.

Standing poised atop the fin, facing his great enemy at last, Bane began to unwrap the other end of the chain from the coil twined around his body. Then, whirling the dangling end overhead, he slashed it like a whip at Batman.

Batman grabbed the grapnel cable and pushed off, swinging to one side. The chain slammed into the funnel behind him, missing him, but leaving a deep indentation where it struck.

At the pinnacle of his swing, Batman hurled a Batarang, which whirled around Bane like a boomerang, trailing a cable behind it. As the Batarang spun, the cable wrapped more and more tightly, pinning Bane's arms to his side, binding the thick linked chain tight against his massive body.

Batman swung at Bane's chest and, kicking out with both feet, knocked the monstrous brute off balance and toppled him off the far side of the fin.

As Bane fell, the long chain, one end of which was still attached to Carleton Duquesne, trailed up over the fin.

In an instant, the chain went taut over the top of the fin, stretched to its full length, with Bane bound and dangling at one end and Duquesne, deep beneath the water, bound and helpless at the other.

Then gravity asserted itself. The massive Bane plummeted toward the deck like a stone, jerking Carleton Duquesne from the water and into the air.

Kathy, who had had her arms around her father in a vain attempt to raise him, was pulled from the water along with him.

Bane's body, bound with Batman's cable, slammed onto the deck below.

Father and daughter, dangling on their chain from the decorative fin, swung in a slow arc twenty-five feet above the ground. A drop to the deck below would mean their certain deaths.

Roaring his fury, Bane stretched out his massive arms and snapped the superstrong Batcable that bound him as if it were the thinnest string.

Then he shrugged off the annoying chains.

Freed of the weight at the other end, Carleton Duquesne and Kathy began to plummet toward the deck below.

But Batman grabbed the sliding chain in his gloved hands. Braced and straining mightily, he jerked them to a stop. Then, hand over hand, he lowered Duquesne and Kathy slowly to the poolside deck.

They're safe, Batman thought. Then realized, *No. It's too late. No one on this ship is safe.*

In the engine room, directly below, the counter on the bomb hit :01, then :00.

There was a bright white flash.

The first explosion blew a hole in the hull and ignited the fuel tanks. Flames, accompanied by thick, noxious smoke, roiled through the hole into the sky.

A second, even larger explosion ripped up through the aft section of the ship, shattering the games deck and sending lifeboats and other equipment flying sky-high.

The shock wave toppled Batman from his perch on the fin. On the deck below, it slammed Bane to his hands and knees.

Once they were out of the water, Kathy had been able to pull one of her father's arms free of the confining chain. Duquesne was shucking off his remaining bonds when the decking on which they had been crouched arched and buckled.

Kathy and her father fell flat as, right beside them, the swimming pool began to collapse into the lower decks.

The whole world tilted dramatically, and Kathy screamed as everything went dark.

37

Billowing fireballs shot from all the hallways attached to the stern and turned the cavernous Atrium into one vast conflagration. The massive skylight dome shattered as the superheated weaponry stored in the lower level began a chain reaction of collateral explosions.

As sections of the decking began to blow apart, Bane's goons rushed to abandon their posts.

The more experienced guards climbed into lifeboats and were lowered to the water. But others dove from the ship and made for the life preservers that littered the bay like carelessly tossed garbage.

The bridge pilot turned to his second in command. "You think maybe we should abandon ship?" he asked.

"Ya think?" his lieutenant asked sarcastically.

Together the pilots deserted the wheelhouse, scrambled for the edge of the ship, and leapt desperately into the water beyond.

* * *

Near the docking bay, where the Penguin and Rupert Thorne faced Rocky and Sonia, sections of the hull exploded.

A shock wave like a wall of solid, toxic heat hit the Batwomen.

Crouched on their gliders, Sonia and Rocky tumbled down and backward toward the water.

Below them, an expanding slick of oil oozed from a ruptured tank. Then hot embers struck the slick, and with a loud *Whumph!* it ignited.

Taking advantage of the pandemonium, the Penguin and Thorne, closer to the water and temporarily more protected, revved the speedboat engine and raced desperately through the burning water toward the shore.

In the tumbling chaos, Rocky had managed to stay aboard her glider. Now, she hovered amid the hellish confusion of noise and stink, trying to get her bearings. Between smoke and fire, explosion and darkness, it was hard to tell what was happening.

She felt heat close by and whirled. To her horror, her cape was on fire. In near panic, she ripped it off, along with her mask, and hurled both into the bay.

She looked around desperately and called in a hoarse voice, "Sonia! Sonia, where are you?"

Miraculously, she spotted her friend lying facedown in the water, lit by nearby pools of burning oil.

Rocky swooped low, then dove from her glider into the filthy water. Blessing the life-saving lessons she'd taken as a teenager, Rocky grabbed Sonia, flipped her over, held her face above the water, and pulled off Sonia's mask and hood. Sonia began to cough and choke on her own as she gasped for air.

Behind them, Rocky heard the sound of a speedboat motor

increasing in volume. It was coming right at them. She looked up, knowing she wasn't going to like what she saw.

The Penguin was steering the speedboat right at the two half-submerged women. Rocky could see that his teeth were clenched with his determination to run them down.

Rocky fingered her belt and thought of calling her Batglider, even as she realized there was no way she could get herself and Sonia on board in time to save them.

Then a gentle swell of water lifted them. And, with a sucking sound, the Batboat emerged from underwater, placing itself protectively between the Penguin's boat and the floating Bat-women.

Seeing a dark and looming shape rise suddenly before him, the Penguin shouted a curse and jerked hard on the wheel. The speedboat swerved dramatically, barely sideswiping the submersible.

"Forget those broads," Thorne shouted. "Just get us out of here!"

Inside the cockpit of the Batboat, Robin hit a button, and his view-port canopy popped open. The teenager leaned out and pulled a dazed Sonia Alcana from Rocky's arms.

"I got her," Robin said.

Sonia looked up at Rocky. "Don't . . . worry about me," she coughed out. "Just get them!"

Rocky nodded. "You got it!"

She thumbed her belt control. In seconds, her Batglider was hovering right above the water. Rocky grabbed hold of the edge and hoisted herself aboard.

With a quick wave at Sonia and Robin, Rocky zoomed off into the night, in hot pursuit of the Penguin and Rupert Thorne.

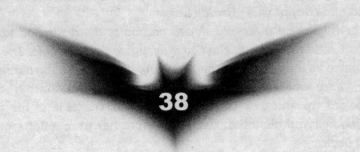

38

Kathy Duquesne awoke, disoriented and uncomfortable. "Where am I?" she mumbled. She ached everywhere and was almost too tired to move.

She was lying—no, hanging, she realized—faceup on a hot, hard surface. But if her back was hot, the bottoms of her feet felt blistered.

She forced open her eyes and looked down. Below, she saw a deep pit rimmed with jagged metal. At its bottom were what must surely be the flames of hell.

"My fault," she said again. "Because I set the bomb... because I killed them all. My... my father!"

She sobbed out a breath that ended in a hacking cough.

Above her head, there was a ripping sound, and suddenly she lurched down toward the burning pit.

Her alarming downward slide brought a flood of adrenaline coursing through her system. In an instant, Kathy was awake and focused.

Then the frightening motion stopped as abruptly as it had begun.

Kathy glanced upward and saw that her cape was snagged

on a splintered deck board. But the jagged hole where the fabric had caught was growing larger.

I'm lying on a steeply sloped section of the destroyed upper deck, she thought, *at close to a forty-five degree angle. The engine room is on fire below me. I'm hanging above it . . . by a thread.*

There was a noise above her, a croaked-out "Kathy." She looked up and saw Carleton Duquesne, the side of his face bloodied and blistered, staring down at her from a flat section of deck.

Their eyes met. Then Duquesne looked away. He inched backward, until he was out of her sight.

Tears welled in her eyes. Her daddy was leaving her, just as her mother had. He was angry. Couldn't forgive her. No longer loved her.

And whose fault is that? her inner voice asked scornfully.

Again the cape ripped, and Kathy slid several inches closer to annihilation.

There was a bumping noise above her head. *Something's falling,* Kathy thought. *It will hit me and take me down with it.* She clamped her eyes shut and began to pray desperately as she waited for the inevitable plunge into the inferno.

"Kathy." She heard her father's commanding croak.

She opened her eyes and saw a life preserver on a rope sliding down the angled wall beside her.

"Grab it!" Duquesne said hoarsely. "Hurry!"

She seized the life preserver, clutched it to her, and looked up to see her father standing on the edge of the destroyed deck, holding the rope in his strong hands.

A ripping sound from overhead told her that her cape had finally torn free. She slid, screaming, down the incline. Then the rope pulled taut and held.

With grunts of effort, her father began to pull up the rope, hand over hand. And slowly, jerkily, Kathy began to rise from the abyss.

Finally, she smiled up at her father.

It's like being born again, she thought. *Like moving from certain death to life.*

"I'm sorry," she whispered. "Daddy, I'm so sorry. For everything."

As their speedboat neared the shore, the Penguin and Rupert Thorne gazed back at their destroyed transport ship.

"It's going down, Penguin," Thorne growled.

Above the sound of the speedboat's motor, the Penguin shouted, "Our only consolation is that it will take a few bat rats with it—"

His assessment was interrupted as a Batangle trailing a cable zipped around their motor. The boat jolted as the cable grew taut.

They looked up.

Rocky on her jet board was being towed at the other end of the cable by their speedboat, as if she were hang gliding.

"Batwoman! Those cursed females have more lives than cats!" the Penguin grumbled. "Cut her loose."

"No!" Thorne said, raising his laser bazooka. "We have this one right where we want her!"

He began to fire short laser bursts, but the jouncing of the speedboat made it difficult to aim.

So far so good, Rocky thought as she dipped and dove to make herself even more difficult to hit. *But I can't keep this up forever.*

A large channel-marking buoy bobbed ahead of her in the water.

Excellent! she thought.

Leaning sideways, she dove down toward the waterline. As she approached the floating marker, she snapped the cable end hook off her glider and attached it to the buoy.

Now separated from the speedboat, she rode her glider skyward.

"Hey, what's she up to?" Rupert Thorne asked.

The cable between the speedboat and the buoy went rigid, jerking the speedboat to an abrupt stop and tearing both the motor and rear end off the racer.

With nothing anchoring them, the Penguin and Thorne pitched off the boat, head over heels into the water.

For an instant, the felons disappeared beneath the swells. Then they bobbed to the surface, scowling and treading water.

"I see you can swim," Rocky called down to them.

"Of course I can swim," the Penguin snapped. "What penguin can't?"

Thorne looked toward the shore, considering his options.

"You can give it a try if you want," Rocky told him coolly. "But a Gotham Harbor Patrol boat is headed this way. You won't get far."

Thorne snorted in disgust and grabbed for an SS *Naiad* life preserver as the police boat pulled alongside.

39

Standing beneath the funnel as fire licked up from the engine room below, Bane punched a button on a wristband, signaling the controls on his belt pack. The regulators there responded, increasing the flow of Venom—a combination of anabolic steroids and liquid nutrients—that surged through the tubes implanted in his body.

Bane took one menacing step toward Batman. Then another. With every step, he grew larger, taller, stronger, more monstrous, and, if possible, more frightening.

He lunged toward Batman with an unearthly roar, arms spread wide to crush him.

Batman glanced around quickly, surveying his situation. Below was an inferno. Above, the funnel, with its platform-like fins, miraculously still held.

He fired a grappling hook up at the near fin.

Bane lunged, barely missing his opponent as the grapnel retracted and Batman was pulled into the air.

As he reached the fin, Batman glanced downward. Directly below, the monstrous Bane was digging his fingertips into the side of the funnel, climbing the near-vertical metal surface as he stalked his chosen prey.

In seconds, Bane had climbed atop the fin. He lunged toward Batman, but Batman dodged him on the narrow platform, then brought both interlocked fists down on Bane's misshapen back.

Bane's grunt was the only sign he had felt the blow.

The super-soldier was not only strong and nearly invulnerable, he was also lightning fast. So far Batman had stayed one step ahead of Bane's sledgehammer blows. But he knew he would soon begin to tire. And any mistake could be his last.

Another explosion rocked the ship, knocking both combatants off balance.

Bane reached out for Batman, who lurched backward, once again avoiding physical contact. But this time, Bane's massive fist closed around the end of Batman's cape. He jerked hard, slamming Batman back against the funnel, and then pulled him forward into a deadly bear hug.

Batman writhed, trying to twist away to keep from getting his back broken. Again Bane slammed the Dark Knight against the funnel, trying to knock him senseless.

Batman kicked his foot hard against the funnel, and Bane stumbled backward, flailing his arms for balance, and sank to his knees at the edge of the narrow platform.

Finally, Batman was able to break free.

He landed in a crouch, then, with a grunt of pain, grabbed for his side. *Best-case scenario,* he thought, *I have several cracked ribs. Worst case...* He didn't want to think about that now.

Bane pushed himself upright, once again towering over the injured Dark Knight.

Then, as Bane grabbed for him again, Batman reached into

his cape pouch and pulled out a shiny metallic blob. For a moment, he held it, then he hurled it at the center of Bane's chest.

"What—" Bane shouted, surprised as the shiny metal struck his sternum. Wirelike tentacles morphed from its shiny surface and rapidly spread around Bane's torso, pinning Bane's massive arms.

Seeing the thinning wires, Bane's surprise turned to contempt. He straightened, straining against the silvery bonds.

"Have you learned nothing, Batman?" he snarled. "No bonds can hold me. Especially puny wires like these."

But as his muscles strained against the tightening cables, the rapidly thinning wires ruptured one tube, then another.

The Venom fluids sprayed from ruptured hoses, and before Batman's eyes, Bane's massive body began to shrink. With every passing second, the super-soldier was losing muscle mass. His strength decreased with every spurt.

"No!" Bane snapped, grim and furious. With a superhuman effort, the monstrous super-soldier shattered the alloy and burst free. Still hemorrhaging liquids, Bane lurched toward Batman. "I can still crush you!" he shrieked.

From the corner of his eye, Batman spotted movement overhead. *The bridge,* he realized.

The momentum of the ship was carrying it under the Gotham Gate Bridge. But without a pilot, the *Naiad* had drifted toward the lower section that abutted the shore.

We're going to ram the bridge, Batman thought. He shouted out a warning: "Bane, look out!"

But Bane was beyond reason. He grabbed for Batman again. Ribs burning, Batman stumbled back, pulled his grappler, aimed it over Bane's head, and fired.

The grappler whooshed through the air, embedded in the left bridge tower, then retracted, jerking Batman over Bane's head, too fast for the diminished Bane to catch him.

Bane spun around, reaching for his enemy, and realized he had a terrible problem. The funnel, including the fin on which he was standing, was too tall to clear the bridge, which was now several inches from his head.

The top of the funnel crashed into the bridge deck.

Automobiles skidded violently on the bridge as it swayed, but held.

The thinner metal of the ship's funnel dented, then was crushed by the force of the impact. Finally, the whole structure began to collapse toward the deck below.

With a shriek of despair, Bane toppled from the fin and fell toward the burning hold.

Another explosion sent a geyser of flames into the air, singeing the bottom of the Gotham Gate Bridge as the destroyed cruise ship passed beneath, sliding from the bay on its final voyage toward the open sea.

40

Batman hung from a cable hooked on to the bridge tower as the *Naiad* passed beneath him. Inhaling the smoke-laden air, he coughed, sending a sharp pain through his chest. His ribs hurt like the devil. But at least he was alive.

If I don't black out and fall to my death, I might even stay alive, he thought. Unfortunately, blacking out seemed a definite possibility. His vision shrunk to a narrow point of light. He felt his hand grow numb. . . .

Suddenly, through the smoke, a shapely figure glided toward him.

"Batman!" Sonia Alcana shouted, relief apparent in her voice. "Are you all right?"

"Sonia," he gasped. "Great. Fine."

"Sure you are," she answered. She lowered her glider until it was right beneath his feet.

"Hop aboard," she told him. "Considering how much help you've been, the least I can do is offer you a ride."

Grateful for her assistance, Batman dropped onto the glider beside her.

"Kathy," Batman said. "She was on the ship! Is she—"

As they dipped toward the water, Rocky whizzed by, smiling. "Kathy's down there," Rocky called out, pointing below.

An exhausted Kathy Duquesne was lying on the bottom of a lifeboat, with her head resting on a life preserver, smiling wanly up at the Batwomen—and Batman—circling above her. Carleton Duquesne was slumped beside her, apparently lost in his own thoughts. But, Batman noted, he had his daughter's hand clasped as if he would never again let it go.

Kathy raised her other hand, wiggling the fingers, and whispered, "Ta-ta!"

The Coast Guard had arrived and were flanking the burning *Naiad* as it moved, more slowly now, through Gotham Bay and out to sea.

Fire ships sprayed the massive ship from several angles. Ambulances lined the shore. And police boats had begun to crowd the bay.

Commissioner Gordon and Sergeant Harvey Bullock leaned forward in the bow of a Gotham City Police cruiser. Bullock trained his binoculars on Batwoman and Batman as they dipped toward the boat on the Batglider.

"Looks like Batwoman's lost the mask," Bullock muttered to Commissioner Gordon. "Let's see who—"

Bullock's mouth fell open, and the toothpick he was chewing dropped from his slack lips. He could hardly believe what his eyes were telling him.

"S-Sonia?" Bullock whispered.

With practiced precision, Sonia Alcana landed her Batglider on the deck of the police boat. Then, with Commissioner Gordon's aid, she helped the injured Batman onto the deck.

"What happened to you?" Gordon asked, his voice hoarse with concern.

"Bane." Batman gasped the answer.

Commissioner Gordon nodded. And shuddered. That one-word answer carried a world of pain. Batman was lucky to be alive.

Bullock stared in shocked silence as Sonia fingered the control on her belt, sending the Batglider to hover in the sky somewhere above.

Seeing the bemused look on Bullock's face, she smiled at him wryly. "Maybe I should write the report this time, eh, Sergeant?" she said.

41

Sonia Alcana pulled out a drawer from her desk, turned it up-side down, and dumped its entire contents—pens, pencils, erasers, paper clips—into a cardboard box. She slid the empty drawer back into the desk.

Police Headquarters, she thought. *The one place I wanted to be.* She sighed heavily and reached for the next drawer down.

She was dressed in civilian clothes now. Not Gotham City blues.

The window beside her desk was open. From outdoors came the shriek of sirens, the rumble of traffic, the roar of Gotham City at night.

She was going to miss it.

"Cleaning out your desk, I see." A familiar voice spoke behind her.

She hesitated for a moment. "Condoning vigilantes is one thing," she said. "But even Commissioner Gordon draws the line at employing them."

She pulled out the second drawer. It was filled with memen-tos of her time with Gotham's finest. A cup given to her by a grateful citizen. A whoopee cushion some practical joker had left on her chair. These she pulled carefully from the drawer and placed in the box individually, as if they were made of gold.

"We're just lucky the DA is looking the other way," she said. She finally glanced at Batman. "Someday you'll have to tell me how you do it. How you keep from crossing the line. When we put on the masks, we couldn't even *see* the line anymore."

Batman folded his arms across his massive chest. "Maybe I don't take it as personally," he said.

Sonia glanced up at him and raised an eyebrow. "Somehow, I doubt that," she said.

They'd gotten their revenge on the villains who had wronged them. Maybe they'd even prevented the bad guys from acts of greater evil. But their actions had been lawless. They had valued revenge too highly and human life not enough. And each had paid a price.

Sonia had lost the job she loved.

Kathy had almost killed her own father, had lost his wealth and her own, and had landed him in jail.

Rocky's torment was more subtle. She had punished the Penguin, but she still had no proof that he had framed her fiancé, Kevin.

Worst of all, the Batwoman caper had convinced Kevin beyond a shadow of a doubt that he was a bad influence, and that association with him would ruin Rocky's life. He had broken off their engagement and had steadfastly refused to see Rocky or even to speak with her again.

Sonia sighed. Only one more drawer to go.

From her top drawer, she pulled out her badge and placed it on her empty desk. She stared at it solemnly.

"The city is losing a good cop," Batman said, then asked, "Where will you go?"

Sonia shrugged. "I'm not sure. Someplace simpler." She

gave him a wry smile. "Where capes aren't the prevailing fashion."

She stood decisively and looked Batman squarely in the face. "Don't tell me you dropped by to wish me luck."

Batman pulled an envelope from his cloak. "That," he said. "And to give you this." He handed the envelope to Sonia.

"It's exculpatory evidence that should help release Dr. Ballentine's fiancé from jail." He smiled crookedly. "I thought it should come from you."

"I—" Sonia's eyes widened in surprise. She looked down at the envelope. In a voice full of unshed tears, she said, "Thank you, Batman. I'm sure she'll appreciate it—"

A sudden breeze ruffled her hair. She looked up, but he had already disappeared through the open window.

She smiled. "I think I'm going to miss that too," she said to the empty room.

42

It had taken a month for the new evidence Batman had uncovered to be presented in the case of Kevin Lee.

It had taken another two months for it to wend its way through the legal system. But now the verdict was in, and the world knew the true story.

A high-tech entrepreneur, Kevin had refused to participate in a money-laundering scheme devised by the Penguin. As an example to anyone else who might consider defying him, the Penguin had framed Kevin Lee for drug smuggling and had tried to ensure that Kevin would spend the next twenty years in prison.

The day Kevin was scheduled to be released from prison dawned crisp and golden. Rocky Ballentine, along with her friend Kathy Duquesne, waited in the brilliant fall sunshine outside the Stonegate Prison main gate.

"I hated who my father was, what he did, the hurt he brought to people," Kathy Duquesne told Rocky. "But what I did . . . why I did it . . ." She trailed off, then began again. "I just wanted what I wanted, and I wouldn't let anyone or anything get in my way. That's not such a great way to be. Selfish, you know? And it made me think that underneath, Daddy and I aren't so different. Now that he's in there—in prison—because of us . . . of me . . . I feel bad." She sighed.

"Don't beat yourself up too much. He's in prison because of what *he did*," Rocky told her.

"Yeah," Kathy said. "He told me that too. And I told *him*—considering the collateral damage from our Batwoman escapade—*we're* lucky *we* didn't end up keeping him *company*!" She sighed.

"Amen to that!" Rocky shook her head. "You know, your dad may have come to hate his life as much as you hated yours."

Kathy looked at her friend, impressed. "For a mad genius, you're pretty smart. At least Daddy and I can talk now.

"For years, you know, he blamed himself for my mom's death. She'd begged Dad to go legit, and to please her, he was making moves in that direction. Another gang took that as a sign of weakness and tried to blow him away . . . and killed her instead.

"Since then, Dad's been afraid to be anything but a tough guy. It gave him an ulcer. . . .

"Having me trailed by bodyguards was just his way of making sure I was safe, his nutty way of showing he loved me. I just didn't understand. I was so angry I didn't *want* to understand."

Kathy smiled crookedly at her friend. "We're not rich anymore. I have to work for a living now.

"And Dad's making a deal to testify against Thorne and the Penguin. It's an adjustment, but I think, in the end, we'll both be happier. . . ."

Enough of this maudlin stuff, Kathy decided in one of her lightning mood switches.

"Change of subject," she announced. "How's the handsome Bruce Wayne?"

Rocky blinked. "Bruce Wayne?"

Kathy rolled her eyes. "Yeah. The good-looking billionaire who signs your paycheck. Your boss?"

Rocky shrugged. "Fine, I guess." Head tilted, she frowned at Kathy. "You haven't heard from him?"

Kathy sighed and looked away. "No. I think he's been reading the papers. . . ."

A questioning voice interrupted their conversation. "Rocky?"

Both women turned to face the prison gate.

Kevin had stepped through the open door. He was pale, but he was wearing a suit. His valuables were in a sack slung over his shoulder. For an instant, he simply stood blinking in the bright sunlight, breathing in freedom.

Then he ran toward his fiancée.

"Rocky!" he shouted in a voice that broke with emotion.

Rocky dashed toward Kevin, arms flung wide.

Then they were in each other's arms.

"It looks like my mission here is done," Kathy whispered to herself. She turned and sauntered toward the parking lot.

Of the three Batwomen, Rocky's motive was the most altruistic, she thought. *She deserves her happily-ever-after ending.*

Suddenly, she stopped in her tracks, not able to believe what she was seeing.

Bruce Wayne was there, sitting on the front fender of the red convertible Kathy had given him on the cliff by the sea.

He raised an eyebrow and mimicked her wave. "Ta-ta!" he said.

For an instant, she just stood there, staring at him.

"Missing a car lately?" he asked. He slid off the fender and opened the passenger door.

As if she were sleepwalking, Kathy stepped forward and slipped into the passenger seat. "What are you doing here?" she asked.

"Funny thing. This morning I got up thinking, 'Something's wrong.' And then I realized—no gunfire, no explosions, no goons out to do me in."

He closed the door, walked around to the driver's side, and climbed in behind the wheel. "Everything was peaceful and quiet, and that's when I realized how much I missed you."

"You poor thing," Kathy said with pseudo-sincerity. She crossed her arms. "But that was the old Kathy Duquesne. The new one is different. She intends to live a life of complete respectability."

"How disappointing," Bruce answered, sounding crestfallen. His expression was appropriately plaintive.

Kathy nodded. "'Fraid so." Then the corners of her mouth twitched, and like a princess graciously granting a blessing, she relented. "Well, maybe an explosion now and then."

Grinning roguishly, Bruce gunned the engine and carried her off to explore the quiet and sunny countryside.

about the author

LOUISE SIMONSON was born in Atlanta, where she attended Georgia State University. Her first job in comics was at Warren Publishing, where she eventually became vice president and senior editor. At Marvel Comics she was an editor of numerous titles, including *Star Wars* and *The Uncanny X-Men*. Simonson left her editorial position to pursue a freelance writing career, creating the award-winning *Power Pack* series. Among other titles she has written are *X-Factor*, *The New Mutants*, and *Web of Spider-Man*. For DC Comics she has scripted *Batman*, *The New Titans*, and *Superman: Man of Steel*. She is also the author of *Superman: Doomsday & Beyond* (Bantam, 1993), *I Hate Superman!* (Little, Brown, 1996), and *Steel* (Troll, 1997), a novelization of the film starring Shaquille O'Neal, based on the character she co-created. She has also written numerous episodes of *The Multipath Adventures of Superman* (presented by Warner Bros. Online, 1999–2002). Louise Simonson lives in upstate New York with her husband, Walter, who is also a writer and artist.

frozen buildings.
chemical spills.
robot umbrellas.

just another night in gotham city...

Join Batman For Two <u>NEW</u> CD-ROM Action Mysteries.

COMING IN SEPTEMBER 2003!

Uncover the clues. Crack the case. Foil the fiends.

Available wherever computer games are sold, at www.learningco.com, or by calling 1-800-822-0312

The Learning Company®